ROGUE ANGEL

Alex Archer

STAFF OF JUDEA

D1407995

A GOLD EAGLE BOOK FROM

WORLDWIDE®

TORONTO • NEW YORK • LONDON
AMSTERDAM • PARIS • SYDNEY • HAMBURG
STOCKHOLM • ATHENS • TOKYO • MILAN
MADRID • WARSAW • BUDAPEST • AUCKLAND

Recycling programs
for this product may
not exist in your area.

First edition March 2013

ISBN-13: 978-0-373-62161-3

STAFF OF JUDEA

Special thanks and acknowledgment to
Joe Nassise for his contribution to this work.

The
LEGEND

The broadsword, plain and unadorned,
gleamed in the firelight. He put the tip against
the ground and his foot at the center of the blade.
The broadsword shattered, fragments falling
into the mud. The crowd surged forward,
peasant and soldier, and snatched the shards
from the trampled mud. The commander tossed
the hilt deep into the crowd.
Smoke almost obscured Joan, but she continued
praying till the end, until finally the flames climbed
her body and she sagged against the restraints.

Joan of Arc died that fateful day in France,
but her legend and sword are reborn....

1

The Monastery at Qumran
68 CE

"Quickly, my brothers!" the rabbi said, watching as the men around him packed the treasure into whatever receptacles they had on hand—clay jars, wooden boxes, rough burlap sacks, anything that could be used to transport it away from the monastery. The scrolls on the library shelves would be next; the precious documents would be placed in clay jars and stored in cliff caves in the wadi nearby.

Time was of the essence. He had received word that the dreaded Legio X Fretensis, the tenth legion of the sea strait, was marching in their direction and under orders to seize anything of value in the name of Titus.

Ordinarily this wouldn't have been a concern. The rabbi and his people had lived under the Roman yoke for years now and had endured more than one visit from the emperor's dogs. Each time it was the same. The troops would search the property, rifling cupboards, smashing crockery and generally making a mess of things. A few of them, including the rabbi, would be beaten or whipped for no better reason than that they were Jews. And then the troops would leave, not having found anything of interest. The rabbi and his followers were a community of scholarly ascetics, studying the Torah and what it meant to be the chosen of God. The only thing of value in the entire complex was the ever-growing collection of religious texts housed in the library, but since the Romans had no interest in the word of God these were always left alone.

These, however, were not ordinary times.

Rumors of change had been spreading for more than a year now. As tensions had risen throughout the spring and the air had grown heavy with talk of revolt and armed conflict, the high priest in Jerusalem had devised a plan to keep the temple treasures out of the hands of the Romans. Little by little the vaults had been emptied, the offerings of the faithful carried by trusted men to the small Essene community on the shores of the Dead Sea at Qumran. There they were delivered into the hands of the rabbi, a childhood friend of the high priest. The rabbi had the treasure cataloged, split into lots and then carried off again under the cover of darkness to hiding places scattered throughout the Negev Desert. Information concerning each cache was inscribed in a pair of scrolls, the first noting the type and location of the wealth, the second providing the necessary clues to correctly interpret the simple code used to obscure the locations in the first document. Both documents were needed to find the treasure. As soon as they were finished here the rabbi intended to make certain that the scrolls were sent to trusted followers in remote parts of the country, there to remain until it was safe.

The latest shipment from Jerusalem had come in four days before and they had barely begun cataloging it when word had reached them of the legion's movement. Even worse, the same message told them that command of Fretensis had passed to Larcius Lepidus, a man known for his brutality and his love of confrontation. Give him half an excuse and Lepidus would burn the place to the ground.

He began urging his people to work faster.

When the scrolls were finished, the rabbi called for a messenger. A young boy of no more than sixteen stepped up, and for a moment all the rabbi could do was blink.

So young, he thought. But then again, perhaps it was for the best. The Roman forces would be looking for one of his usual couriers, not this boy. And who was he to decide how a man—any man, young or old—should offer his life in the name of duty and faith?

The boy it would be.

"What is your name, son?" he asked.

"Jonathan, Rabbi."

Jonathan. A good omen, that.

"Do you know what to do, Jonathan?"

The youth nodded. "I am to take the scroll to Elazar ben Yair at Masada. I am to give it to him personally and to no one else."

The rabbi nodded. "And?"

Jonathan's expression hardened but the rabbi was pleased that the boy did not waver as he said, "No matter what happens, I must not let myself or the scroll be captured by the Romans. I must destroy the scroll and sacrifice myself if necessary to prevent this."

"Let us hope it does not come to that, eh?" He handed over the scroll, written on bronze.

Before the boy could respond, the door on the other side of the room burst open. It was Ephram, one of his senior disciples. The room's light revealed the panic on the man's face.

"The Romans are less than an hour's march from the gates!" he cried.

So little time. The rabbi scolded himself. They would have time; the Lord would provide.

The rabbi turned back to the messenger, said a quick prayer over him and sent him on his way. He would either make it or he wouldn't. It was out of the rabbi's hands.

That took care of one of the scrolls, but the rabbi still had to deal with the second. He had intended to send a second messenger out by a different route in a few hours, but his plan had been predicated on the legion taking longer to reach them. Sending both scrolls out by messenger at the same time was far too risky.

He could afford to have the Romans seize the first of the scrolls—without the second, the first was all but useless—but letting them get their hands on both was unthinkable. He would have to secure it much closer to home, for the time being, and hope he survived long enough to move it to a safer location. He pondered the problem for a moment and then decided that he would secret the copper scroll with the rest of the library texts that were even now being hidden in the caves of the wadi above the complex. It was unlikely the Romans would take the time to search there and the scroll would be protected from the elements.

The rabbi called to several of his men and instructed them on what he wanted done.

IT WAS JUST AFTER dawn when the Romans were sighted approaching the eastern gate of the Qumran complex. A few of the faithful remained with the rabbi, those who had refused his order to leave while they still had time to do so. They stood with him now just inside the gates, waiting for the arrival of the legion, and he was profoundly grateful for their presence.

It didn't take long.

The first squad of foot soldiers rushed in and took up defensive positions facing them. It was always this way.

The real threat would be arriving momentarily.

The rabbi had never laid eyes on Larcius Lepidus but he knew him the moment he came in through the gate. Unlike most of the other Roman generals the rabbi had encountered in the past, this one did not stand on politics or ceremony. Where other generals had arrived in gleaming chariots or on magnificent horses, this one walked in like a common foot soldier, and indeed, he even resembled one in his arms and armor. The authority that surrounded him left little doubt that he was far more than that, however. The phalanx of troops parted before him like a cresting wave as he walked over and surveyed the men assembled before him, giving the rabbi time to study him in turn.

He was of average height, with a hard, uncompromising face and a sharp beak of a nose. A scar marked his left cheek.

"Who is in charge here?" he asked.

The rabbi stepped forward.

Lepidus glared at him. "Where is the treasure?"

The rabbi frowned. "We are a scholarly community with—"

That was as far as he got. Lepidus's mailed fist crashed into the side of his face, sending him to the ground.

"Do not lie to me, Jew! I know the temple wealth is here, somewhere. Save yourself and your men and tell me where it is."

Ignoring the blood dripping from his nose, the rabbi climbed to his feet and faced his tormentor. Even if he was inclined to tell the Roman what he wanted to know, which he most emphatically was not, admitting anything at this point was tantamount to treason. They would be tried, found guilty and crucified as enemies of the Empire.

"I do not know of any treasure," the rabbi said.

A savage blow to the temple dropped him like a sack of dates. Darkness beckoned, but the general's next words cut through the haze like a torch in the night.

"Burn it!" Lepidus cried. "Burn it all!"

2

"I'm sorry, but we couldn't possibly take less than five." Annja Creed stared dispassionately at the three men seated across the table from her, taking care to hide even the slightest hint of emotion. The item she was selling, an ossuary clearly of Jewish manufacture that contained the bones of a Roman soldier, was an oddity, all right, but wasn't worth anywhere close to that price, she knew. The question was, did they?

The flight from New York to Jerusalem had taken twelve hours but she'd arrived the day before the meeting, giving her plenty of time to get acclimated to the time difference. She had awoken this morning, eager to face the challenge of dealing with the three gentlemen seated before her now.

She was not what they had expected. That much had been obvious when they had entered the room and practically fallen over one another in surprise when they found a woman waiting for them. It was precisely the reaction she and Roux, her sometime mentor, sometime partner, had been hoping for.

"They've no doubt spent hours studying what little information they can find on me, working out complicated strategies to deal with any possible move I might make in the negotiation," he'd said when she reached him by phone earlier that morning. "Having you handling things will force them to throw all their carefully crafted plans right out the window. They'll be off balance and scrambling to come up with a response. That's when we'll strike!"

And strike they had. Now it just remained to see if the fish took the bait.

The fish in question were named Cummings, Mortimer and Finch. Lawyers. High-priced ones at that. They were here representing the interests of Mitchell Connolly, the buyer who had contacted Roux several weeks ago with an interest in his ossuary. Annja had done her share of homework, too, after Roux had asked her to handle negotiations on his behalf. Connolly was the man behind a global empire built on mining rights and the exploitation of natural resources. He wasn't as rich as Roux or Garin Braden, not by a long shot, but then again, he hadn't had five hundred years to acquire his wealth the way those two had. Connolly was known to be both a savvy businessman and a cunning negotiator. It was this reputation, more than anything else, which had prompted Annja to accept Roux's invitation to represent him. For someone as highly competitive as she was, the opportunity to pit herself against a man of Connolly's reputation was one she just couldn't resist.

She knew that as a collector Connolly was primarily interested in artifacts from the Roman occupation of Israel, most notably those from the First and Second Temple periods. The ossuary Roux was offering to sell had been dated to the year 50 CE, plus or minus a few decades, so it fit within that general time frame rather nicely. The fact that the bones inside it had been identified as European rather than Middle Eastern was what made the artifact unusual and, more than likely, had triggered Connolly's interest.

Unfortunately, the media mogul must have come up with the same strategy Roux had, sending these three to negotiate in his place.

"Five million? Surely, you're joking, Ms. Creed," Cummings said, glancing at his two companions with a smug little smile. "We aren't prepared to offer anything even close to that ballpark."

Annja looked at them without saying anything. Cummings and Mortimer appeared to have been cut from the same cloth—large, overweight men in expensive suits. Both oozed arrogance, their expressions and body language telling her all she needed to know about their opinion of her. Finch, on the other hand, was the Laurel to their Hardy. Tall and thin, he was dressed in a dark suit that unfortunately made him look more like an old-time undertaker than a lawyer. To Annja's surprise he seemed embarrassed by his colleagues. Apparently he hadn't been at this long enough to build up the same kind of insufferable ego.

Handling this sale for Roux was a nice diversion from *Chasing History's Monsters*. The cable television program on ancient mysteries and legends that she co-hosted had grown in popularity over the past year. The program's climb up the ratings chart had driven the need for new material, and her producer, Doug Morrell, had been all too happy to send her crisscrossing the globe to get it. In the process she'd managed to be involved with some groundbreaking discoveries and her status in the archaeological community had risen along with her popularity as a television star. The long hours and constant travel had been worth it, in that regard, but she was thankful that Roux had come along when he did. She hadn't spent much time in Israel and she was looking forward to a few days to see the sights.

It seemed she was going to get to that sightseeing quicker than expected.

"I guess we're finished, then," she told them in the same unemotional tone she'd been using, and began to collect her things from the table.

There was a moment of silence, broken at last by Cummings. "What are you doing?" he asked in a strangled tone.

Annja looked up, the files in her hand half in and half out of her briefcase. Cummings looked like a fish out of water. It was all she could do to keep from laughing.

"Mr. Cummings, you indicated that your client is not interested in paying anywhere near what my client is asking. That is, of course, your right. As a result, I am exercising my right to end these negotiations. I came here in good faith to sell this artifact. You, apparently, came here to waste everyone's time. I don't believe we have anything more to discuss. Good day, gentlemen."

Chew on that, you bloated toad.

No one said anything as she finished putting her files in the slim leather briefcase Roux had given her that morning and stepped away from the table. She headed for the door of the hotel's conference room, counting silently in her head.

One one thousand, two one thousand, three one thousand...

Behind her, a phone rang.

Gotcha!

"A moment, please, Miss Creed." She turned to find Finch watching her, the still-ringing cell phone in his hand.

Interesting. Perhaps Finch is more of a senior player than I thought. Annja waved him to answer the call.

Finch did so, listening to whoever was on the other end of the line—Connolly most likely. After saying a few words too quietly for Annja to hear, he hung up.

He turned to face her. "Please forgive my colleague, Ms. Creed. In his excitement to do his job, it appears he misspoke."

Annja raised an eyebrow. "Is that so?"

"Perhaps you'd be willing to return to the table so we can discuss this further?"

Cummings looked like he'd swallowed half a dozen lemons, which delighted her to no end, and she took a perverse pleasure in returning to the table and facing Finch rather than his portly partner.

"Mr. Connolly says he is willing to offer three and a half million in cash, as well as a fourteenth-century codex written by the blind monk Justinian in exchange for the ossuary. What do you say to that?"

Annja pretended to give the matter some thought, but already knew she was going to accept the offer. Roux would be lucky to get two million if he offered the ossuary on the open market, so anything over that was pure gravy. With an extra 1.5 million in cash *and* the codex thrown in, it was a deal she couldn't refuse.

After a few moments she pretended to come to a decision, smiled a shark's smile across the table at her opponent and said, "I'd say we have a deal, Mr. Finch."

AN HOUR LATER Annja was sitting in a chaise longue on the balcony of Roux's suite in the David Citadel Hotel. Jerusalem's Old City splayed out before her, the white walls washed bloodred in the setting sun. Roux was seated beside her in the twin to her lounge. He was dressed in light cotton trousers and an open-necked shirt. Comfortable lounging clothes, as he liked to call them.

Annja never would have guessed how her life would

change upon meeting Roux. Nor, she imagined, would he. They had first encountered each other in the foothills of France where Annja had been hunting for information on the legendary Beast of Gevaudan. An irate crime boss out for revenge and an earthquake had thrown the two of them together unexpectedly. The quake had opened the earth under Annja's feet, dragging her into a sinkhole connected to a series of caverns. In the caverns she'd found an irregularly shaped coin hanging on a leather thong around the neck of the man who had died killing the beast's savagery.

The "coin" had turned out to be the last missing piece to the blade of a sword that had once belonged to Joan of Arc. Roux had been there the day the young woman he had sworn to protect, Joan herself, burned in a heretic's fire. He had watched as the sword she had carried had been broken beneath the boot heel of an English captain. The death of the bearer and the sundering of the blade had sparked some kind of mystical working on both Roux and his squire, Garin Braden. It wasn't long after that the two men had discovered their lives had been indefinitely extended. As a result, they had individually begun a search for the pieces of the blade—Roux under the belief that bringing them back together might release him from the weapon's curse, while Braden sought to safeguard his longevity by keeping them out of his former master's hands. The situation had put them on opposing sides for several centuries, until Roux had finally succeeded in bringing all of the pieces of the sword back together again in Annja's presence. To their surprise, the weapon had been mystically forged anew and had become bound to Annja in a fashion no one, not even Roux, had ever imagined.

Thinking of the sword brought a smile to Annja's lips. She could still remember Roux's shock when the blade had reformed right before their eyes. Roux wasn't surprised very often, she'd learned since, but he certainly had been then.

"Is that smile for your victory or the sizable commission you'll be getting as a result?" Roux asked.

"Neither, actually. Just enjoying the day."

"Bah! When you get to my age, they all tend to blend together. But the thrill of besting your adversary never gets old!"

Annja laughed. If there was one constant with Roux, it was that he loved besting anyone he saw as his competition.

"What's on the agenda now that you've milked Connolly out of an extra million?"

"I'm off to Monte Carlo first thing in the morning," Roux answered with a gleam in his eye. "There's a Texas Hold'em tournament beginning tomorrow night that I have every intention of winning. Care to join me?"

She was tempted. Time spent with Roux was always an education of one sort or another. The man had lived for over five hundred years and had seen some of the most amazing changes in human history. She even had money to spare for a change. But it had been some time since she'd last visited Jerusalem and she felt the pull of the Old City.

"I think I'll stay here for a few days," she told him, "take in some of the sights."

There was something here for her in the Old City. She didn't know what yet, but she would soon enough. She'd learned to trust her instincts since taking up the sword and right now every fiber in her being was telling her that she was needed here.

3

After breakfast the next morning, Annja decided to begin her sightseeing expedition by looking at some old books. Two-thousand-year-old books, to be precise. A taxi brought her to the Givat Ram neighborhood in central Jerusalem where many of Israel's important national institutions were located, including the Knesset, the Israeli Supreme Court, the National Library of Israel and the Israeli Museum.

She was headed to the latter, specifically the wing of the museum known as the Shrine of the Book. Built in 1965, the shrine was home to several major archaeological finds, including the Aleppo Codex and the Dead Sea Scrolls. While any of the exhibits would likely have held her interest on any given day, Annja had specifically come to see a showing of the Copper Scroll currently on loan from the Jordanian Museum. The scroll was only rarely on display and Annja was determined to see it while she had the chance.

After all, it isn't every day you get to see a two-thousand-year-old treasure map!

The shrine's architectural design was unusual. Two-thirds of the main structure was underground with the remainder topped by a large white dome reflected in the pool of water that surrounded it. Across from the dome was a black basalt wall. The colors and shapes of the building had been deliberately chosen to suggest the imagery of the War Between the Sons of Light and the Sons of Darkness—the white symbolized the light and the black the darkness. The images came from the scroll, one of those many found in the caves at Qumran and which eventually had become known the world over as the Dead Sea Scrolls. It detailed a battle between the forces of good and the forces of evil. Since taking up the sword, Annja herself had become a living symbol of the struggle between good and evil and she found herself musing over that particular irony as she gazed at the glistening white surface of the dome.

The Dead Sea Scrolls were a collection of over nine hundred biblical texts and other manuscripts that had been discovered in a series of caves in the Qumran wadi between 1947 and 1956. Written on parchment, papyrus and, in the case of the unique scroll she had come to see today, copper. They were some of the oldest surviving copies of certain books from the Hebrew Bible and as such had tremendous historical and religious significance. They were generally divided into three groups—biblical manuscripts, apocryphal or noncanonized biblical texts and sectarian manuscripts. Both the War Scroll and the Copper Scroll were considered sectarian.

Since the fragility of the scrolls made it impossible to keep them on display, various copies were rotated into the display cases housed in the underground portion of the building. Annja descended the stairs to the main floor and began moving through the exhibition, slipping past small groups of tourists. At first she stopped occasionally to examine one display or another, but her impatience finally got the better of her and she moved directly toward the last exhibit, the one featuring the unique scroll she came here to see.

The Copper Scroll.

Besides the fact that it was the only one that had been written on a sheet of metal, what made the scroll so different from the others found at Qumran was that it was not a literary work, but rather a list of sixty-four locations where various items of silver and gold had supposedly been hidden. And not just a few coins here and there, Annja mused, but treasure measured in tons. Back in 1960 the entire haul had been estimated to be worth more than one million U.S., which, she knew, meant it was worth one heck of a lot more now.

So far no one had been able to find any of the various troves listed on the scroll, for the starting point referenced in the directions had either been deliberately obscured or simply lost in the centuries since the scrolls had been written. And *that,* of course, was what made it so intriguing to Annja. The scroll was a giant puzzle just waiting for someone like her to solve.

One thing was for certain, whoever solved it was going to be set for life, if the amount of the treasure listed on the scroll turned out to be accurate.

Annja turned a corner and there at last was the scroll. It had originally been discovered as two separate scrolls written on rolled sheets of copper, but the metal had been too corroded to be unrolled without damaging them so they had been cut lengthwise into twenty-three separate sheets. Several of those sheets hung in the cases before her and she spent some time examining them, marveling at the technology that allowed a voice from the past to travel so far into the future. It was discoveries like this that had prompted her to become an archaeologist and she still found, all these years later, that it was the first true love of her life.

An English translation of the scroll hung on the wall next to the display case. She read the first few lines of the first column.

In the ruin that is in the valley of Acor, under the steps, with the entrance at the East, a distance of forty cubits: a strongbox of silver and its vessels, with a weight of seventeen talents.

Each verse of the scroll held to the same basic formula: general location, specific location and listing of what would be found there.

She looked over at the second column.

In the salt pit that is under the steps: forty-one talents of silver. In the cave of the old washer's chamber, on the third terrace: sixty-five ingots of gold.

Annja knew that a talent was estimated to be about equal to something between fifty and seventy-five pounds, so a single talent worth of gold at today's market prices was worth something in the neighborhood of $800,000. Which means that first verse alone is worth a small fortune to whoever finds it, she thought. And there are sixty-three more locations!

That was a lot of money.

Of course, finding it was the trick. That second verse was a prime example of the problems would-be treasure hunters had with the document. You were supposed to find the salt pit under the steps, but the document didn't give any sense of what building those steps were in. The same held true for the old washer's chamber mentioned a few lines later. It was worse than trying to find a needle in a haystack, because first you had to find the correct haystack!

It made an intriguing puzzle, there was no doubt about that.

Annja was about to move on to the next display when a reflection in the glass of the case next to her caught her eye. She saw a man leaning around the edge of the doorway behind her, a camera in his hand. Normally Annja wouldn't have given it a second thought. They were in a museum and people took pictures in museums. But she was standing squarely in front of the display case, blocking the camera's view of the scroll, which meant the guy was either a completely incompetent photographer or he was taking a picture of *her*.

Annja relished her privacy, perhaps more than most given the unusual nature of the activities she'd become involved in since taking up the sword and the cause that came with it, and she didn't take kindly to having it violated.

She spun around, intending to have a word with her newfound admirer, only to find the words sticking unspoken in her throat when she discovered the newcomer was now holding a gun rather than a camera.

A gun that was pointing directly at her.

4

Fifteen feet.

That was all that separated Annja from the gunman, but it might as well have been fifty. By the time she called her sword and crossed that short distance, the man with the gun would have been able to pull the trigger two, maybe even three times.

I'm quick, but not that quick.

The average person off the street would have been frozen with fear at having a gun pointed in their direction, but not Annja. Her work as bearer of Joan of Arc's sword had brought her into contact with some very hard men and women over the past years, some of whom had appeared far more frightening than the slim, Arab-looking individual standing on the other side of the room, though Annja knew that looks could be deceiving. She would have to be careful, there was no doubt about that, but where another's thoughts might have been mired in indecision by the sight of the gun, Annja was already calculating her options.

She was either going to have to close with him or escape in the opposite direction. Unfortunately, a quick glance showed her that the only door out of the gallery was on the other side of the room, behind the gunman.

Perhaps she could just yell for help?

He must have realized what she was thinking. "I will shoot if you yell, Ms. Creed," he said, betraying British-accented English and the knowledge that he knew exactly who she was.

The first revelation was incidental—probably half the men his age spoke English with a British accent, given the long years that this part of the world had been under British rule. The second revelation was far more interesting. It told her he hadn't come here to rob some random, unsuspecting tourist. He'd been looking specifically for her.

"If you shoot you'll bring security running," she told him, betting that discovery would be the last thing he wanted.

In reply, he twitched the gun to the left and pulled the trigger.

There was a soft, spitting sound and then Annja felt a breath of superheated air race across her cheek as the bullet sped past with only inches to spare. It made more noise thudding into the wall somewhere behind her than it did leaving the barrel of the gun.

"That may be the case, Ms. Creed," the gunman said to her in response, "but you will be dead before they get here."

Annja frowned. She hadn't noticed the silencer on first glance and that wasn't like her. She needed to pay better attention. Her life depended on it.

"What do you want?" she asked, keeping her voice down. A calm gunman was more likely to stay in control, she reasoned, and less likely to shoot the first tourist that happened to wander into their tête-à-tête.

Now if she could just get him to move closer....

"You are about to be offered a job. My colleagues and I would like to discuss why it is not a good idea for you to accept the position. We're going to walk out of here together, without making a fuss. A car will pick us up outside."

"And if I choose not to cooperate?"

"Then I will step back into the gallery behind me and start shooting civilians until you change your mind. We intend to have a conversation, one way or another. It is up to you."

He could have been commenting on the weather or some other banality rather than killing innocent people in cold blood. Hearing that tone was enough to convince her he was deadly serious.

He wasn't giving her much of a choice, now was he?

"Lead on," she said with what she hoped was a disarming smile.

He didn't register the humor in her remark. He gestured for her to come toward him, stepping back out of the way as she drew closer, keeping himself out of her reach.

She couldn't fault him for his caution. She *did* intend to go for his gun, just not in the way he expected. She made note of the waist-high display case directly behind him and smiled to herself at the way he'd unintentionally eliminated one direction of retreat.

He tensed as she drew abreast and then relaxed slightly as she passed. That was what she was waiting for, that moment when he thought the height of danger had passed.

Annja mentally reached into the otherwhere, that mystical place she'd been made aware of when she'd taken up Joan's sword, and called the weapon to her. The ancient broadsword leaped into her hand as if it possessed an intelligence of its own. The hilt fitted her grip exactly and the weapon seemed perfectly balanced, as if it had been made for her and her alone.

As the sword flashed into existence, Annja spun to one side and lashed out with the weapon, aiming for the arm that was holding the handgun. She could have taken his hand off at the wrist, and probably should have, but something caused her to turn the blade at the last minute. Instead of slashing through flesh and bone, the flat of the blade caught the fingers of the hand holding the gun, knocking the weapon from the gunman's grasp.

He surprised her by recovering almost immediately. Even as she was bringing the sword back around for another strike, he spun around and delivered a near-perfect ax kick to her shoulder, the heel of his foot hammering into the nerve junction near her collarbone and causing the arm holding the sword to go numb. The sword clattered to the floor and Annja willed it away into the otherwhere as she skipped backward, out of reach of another strike.

Watch it. He's quick and he knows what he's doing.

He hesitated, clearly confused as he searched the floor for her sword.

Her right arm was still numb, useless for a few seconds, but that didn't stop her from pushing the attack once more while her opponent was still trying to work things out in his head. She lashed out with a savage front kick, followed immediately with a roundhouse punch with her good arm to his head. She'd been training for years prior to becoming the bearer of the sword and she was confident in her ability to handle herself. If she could just delay him long enough, one of the other museum patrons was sure to report their confrontation to security.

Her opponent, however, apparently realized this, as well. He quickly parried her attacks while trying to maneuver into a position where he might be able to incapacitate her long enough to disappear into the crowd in the large atrium beyond.

The gunman threw a left at her face while at the same time targeting her knee with a short, sharp side kick. Annja pulled her head back, letting the fist slide past less than an inch in front of her nose. She turned slightly and raised her leg, taking the kick on the side of her thigh. It hurt, a lot, but it was far better than letting him pulverize her kneecap.

The constant shifting and maneuvering for position had put them several feet from their original positions and Annja now found herself being forced on an angle to the entrance of the gallery, so she only became aware of the fact that they were no longer alone when a man suddenly bellowed, "What the hell's going on here?"

The sound startled her, breaking her concentration for the barest of moments. That split second was all her opponent needed.

Stepping forward, inside her reach, he caught one of her hands in both of his. Pivoting sharply on one foot, he twisted around and heaved her over his shoulder in a classic judo throw. Her momentum carried her several feet across the floor until she fetched up hard against one of the display cases with a loud crash.

From her position on the floor she watched the gunman turn toward the newcomer, a tall, dark-haired man in the casual clothes of a tourist who looked familiar, though she couldn't say why. The gunman delivered a hard right to the man's solar plexus, paralyzing his diaphragm and sending him to the floor as he fought for breath. A glance over the gunman's shoulder revealed several museum patrons headed in their direction.

She had to end this and end it quickly.

As Annja scrambled to her feet, her opponent turned to the display case next to him, raised his elbow and brought it down into the top of the case. Alarms began to howl as the glass shattered beneath the impact of the blow but the gunman didn't seem to notice as he reached inside the case and withdrew the ancient clay tablet inside.

Annja was horrified, far more so now than when he'd been pointing a gun at her head. The tablet in his hands was no doubt thousands of years old and to see him handling it with bare hands made her want to scream. Oil from his fingers could cause incalculable damage to the artifact.

What he did next was worse.

He smiled, said, "Catch," and then threw the tablet about forty-five degrees to her right.

"No!" Annja was first and foremost an archaeologist and something deep inside cried out for her to save the tablet. All thought of stopping the gunman was forgotten as she leaped for it.

Someone, somewhere, must have been watching over that tablet. As Annja hit the floor on her stomach, sliding forward, she managed to catch the fragile piece before it could smash against the unyielding surface of the floor.

Bernie Williams, eat your heart out! she thought as she came to a stop against a display case like a baseball player against the center field wall. She tore her gaze away from the tablet she held gingerly and looked up in time to see the gunman snatch his gun off the floor and slip out past the small crowd that was beginning to gather near the entrance.

Oh, no, you don't.

Laying the tablet carefully on the floor, she jumped to her feet and took off after the gunman. The crowd parted before her as she reached them and she ran forward into the larger atrium, turning this way and that as she tried to find him.

Come on, come on, where did you…there!

She caught a glimpse of him as he approached a door on the far side of the atrium and headed in that direction, trying not to draw too much attention to herself. He was walking at a brisk pace but she knew she'd be able to catch up with him provided she didn't do anything to spook him. All she had to do was keep from giving herself away.

"There she is!" someone shouted from behind her. "That's her!"

Annja turned and found herself staring down the barrel of a pistol for the second time that day. This time, the gun was in the hands of a museum security guard who looked like he was just begging for a reason to use it. A young man stood beside the guard, and, as Annja watched, he jabbed his finger in her direction. "That's the woman who tried to steal the tablet!"

This is so not my day.

She raised her hands over her head, glancing over to where she had seen the gunman. The door he'd been headed for was just shutting behind him and Annja knew she had lost her one chance of catching him. It was going to take hours to work through this mess with the police, and by the time she convinced them they were chasing the wrong individual, the gunman would be long gone.

With a sigh, she turned her attention back to the guard. It was going to be a long afternoon.

The day had one more surprise in store for her, however. When the guard led her back to the gallery to await his superiors, she found the man who had tried to help her calmly talking to several men in finely tailored suits. Annja pegged them as senior museum officials. As she approached, her rescuer turned and said, "Ah, here's Ms. Creed now. I'm certain she'll back up everything I've said."

Annja glanced quizzically at him, wondering how he knew who she was, and then realized with a start that she knew him, as well. Or rather, knew of him. They hadn't met personally but she'd been studying him and his business strategies for the past several days.

The man who had come to her aid was none other than Mitchell Connolly.

5

Her guess had been correct; the men in suits turned out to be the head of security and one of the museum directors. They took her aside and asked her to explain her side of the story. She told them the truth—how she'd come to see the Copper Scroll exhibit, how the gunman had waited until she was alone in the gallery before attempting to abduct her. She had no intention of mentioning the "extracurricular" activities she'd been involved in since taking up the sword, so when she was asked why she thought she had been a target she fell back on a reason as old as the city in which she stood. She was a good-looking woman alone in a foreign place and must have seemed an easy target.

Her story must have matched up with whatever Connolly had told them, because their attitude toward her quickly moved from suspicion to solicitousness. They thanked her for saving the tablet and offered to have their medical staff check her over for injuries, which she declined. As they waited for the police to arrive,

Annja took a moment to speak to her would-be rescuer, who was sitting on a folding chair a few yards away.

"Thank you for getting involved, Mr. Connolly," she said after walking over to stand next to him. "Most people wouldn't have had the courage to."

He rose to his feet and waved away her thanks with a self-conscious grin. "It was the least I could do, Ms. Creed. Couldn't leave a fellow American in distress, now could I?"

"I guess not," she said with a laugh. "It was fortunate that you were here to help."

"Well, I must confess that it wasn't entirely by accident, Ms. Creed."

"Oh?"

"I stopped by your hotel this morning, looking to speak to you, and the concierge told me you'd just left for the museum. As I'd been meaning to see the exhibit myself, I thought I'd kill two birds with one stone."

Annja thought back to when she'd left the hotel that morning. Had she told anyone where she was going? Ah. She had asked for directions to the museum.

"What was it you wanted to speak to me about?"

"I was impressed with the way you handled the negotiations yesterday. So much so that I'd like to discuss a particularly urgent situation I believe you are well-suited to assist me with."

Annja was already shaking her head. "I'm sorry, Mr. Connolly—"

He put a hand on her arm. "Please, Mitchell is fine."

She tried again. "I'm sorry, Mitchell, but my schedule for the next few months is rather tight and I'm not sure I can fit anything else in."

He flashed a smile. "At least hear me out. Let's discuss it over dinner this evening, if you don't have any plans? I assure you it will be worth your while. I wouldn't bother you with trivialities."

Annja thought it over for a moment. The truth was that her schedule really wasn't full at all. In fact, she was kind of surprised at herself for her automatic rejection of his offer. Connolly's wealth wasn't an issue for her. After hanging out with Roux and Garin Braden for so long—who had to be among the world's wealthiest, given how their fortunes stretched back over five hundred years of investments—she had grown, if not comfortable, at least capable of moving in the rarified circles of the extremely wealthy. A point in his favor, the meal would no doubt be absolutely exquisite. If there was one thing Annja appreciated, a fine-cooked meal was it.

A fresh commotion at the entrance of the gallery heralded the arrival of the police and Annja knew their time was up.

She was going to need to unwind after all this and a fine meal sounded like just the ticket.

"All right," she said suddenly. "Dinner, it is."

"Excellent! How about Canela, say around seven?"

Annja hid her smile at the mention of one of Jerusalem's top five restaurants. After all, it was nothing less than she'd expected. "Canela, then," she said. "I look forward to it."

CONNOLLY'S LAWYER MET him at the police station, expediting procedure, and less than an hour later he stepped out the door into the afternoon sunshine. His driver was standing beside his limousine and, after thanking his attorney, the mining magnate gratefully slid inside the cool interior. The charade at the station had been necessary, but he was tired of wasting time and was ready to get back to work.

Connolly pulled out his cell phone and arranged a meeting not far from the Knesset building.

Traffic was light and they reached the desired location inside of fifteen minutes. Connolly instructed his limousine driver to pull the vehicle over to the curb and wait. The car had barely come to a stop before the back door opened and the bearded gunman from the museum slid in opposite Connolly and pulled the door shut behind him.

As the driver got under way again, the newcomer reached up and tugged off the beard he was wearing, revealing the clean-shaven face of Martin Grimes, Connolly's senior exec and right-hand man.

"Damn, that thing itches," Grimes said absently as he took an alcohol-soaked cloth out of a plastic bag lying on the seat next to him and used it to wipe the leftover adhesive off his face.

Connolly waited for him to finish and then asked, "What happened?"

"What happened?" Grimes repeated. "She tried to take my arm off with a sword, that's what happened."

Connolly frowned. "A sword?"

"Yes, a sword," Grimes answered, reacting to the doubtful tone in his employer's voice. "A freakin' medieval broadsword, if you want to be exact."

"Tell me."

Grimes did. Connolly listened without interruption, and sat back to think it over once Grimes was finished. The whole story was incredible. A sword that was there one minute and gone the next. If they had been discussing anyone else Connolly would have dismissed it as hogwash, but he'd heard some interesting rumors regarding the Creed woman and part of today's exercise had been to see if there was any truth to them. Connolly had known Grimes for too many years to think he was making the story up. If he said he saw a sword, then that's exactly what he saw.

"Could she have snatched it from a nearby display case, perhaps?" Connolly asked, doing the reasonable thing and looking for a logical explanation.

Grimes shook his head. "The Shrine of the Book is devoted exclusively to the scrolls recovered at Qumran. They don't even display the camphora jars that many of them were discovered in, never mind any other artifacts. Weapons would be entirely out of the question."

Nor could she had secreted it on her person and carried it into the museum. The entrances were protected by metal detectors. Grimes had been forced to hide the silencer inside a cane he'd ditched once he'd made it inside and had then stolen the gun he'd used from the locker of an off-duty security guard.

How...interesting. Connolly turned the situation over again in his mind.

He was walking a tightrope with this one and he knew it. Later that evening he was going to ask Ms. Creed to lead an extremely important expedition and his decision to do so hadn't been made lightly. Her reputation was unparalleled. If you wanted to find something that history had done its best to make the world forget, then Annja Creed was the one you wanted in charge of your team. Her archaeological successes in recent months had been astounding. Even more important in his eyes was her seemingly natural affinity for artifacts of an unusual nature. It was that...connection...for lack of a better word, that made him want to bring her on board.

This morning they'd tested Creed's reactions under pressure. Connolly was not the type to leave anything to chance. He also wanted to play a bit of reverse psychology on her. By having Grimes confront her, and warn her off accepting the expedition before it had even been offered to her, he wanted to generate a deeper level of interest and make her more inclined to accept when they did sit down to discuss it. Neither of them had expected the woman to be as resourceful as she had so obviously turned out to be and they'd been forced to improvise to provide Grimes with a way out of the situation she'd put them in.

The treasure they were going after was vast. But hidden within that treasure was an even greater one, an object whose value was simply incalculable by modern standards. He intended to make that object his own and he believed that Annja Creed could help him do so. Now he wondered if another perhaps equally valuable object might already be in her possession. It certainly bore thinking about.

"I don't see how we can solve the sword issue at the moment. Keep your eyes open, and perhaps we'll uncover a little something extra to go with our search for the staff. In the meantime I want people watching her hotel to see if she meets with that pain-in-the-ass Roux again. She and I will be dining at Canela tonight at seven, so have your people there at least a half hour in advance. I don't want anymore surprises like we had today."

"Understood."

Grimes rapped on the privacy partition separating them from the driver and a moment later the car pulled to the curb and he got out. He shut the door behind him and walked quickly away without a backward glance.

As the driver pulled away from the curb, Connolly's thoughts returned to Annja Creed and her mysterious sword. He had a hunch he would see it again before their adventure was concluded....

6

Annja arrived at the restaurant promptly at seven. She'd spent several hours at the police station that afternoon, just as she'd expected, but hadn't been able to pinpoint her assailant in any of the hundreds of mug shots. The police had repeatedly asked if there was any reason for someone to target her, but she'd stuck to her original story, leaving them little to go on. It wasn't that she didn't want her assailant to be caught—she did—she just didn't want the police to pry into her life any more than necessary. Thankfully no one had reported seeing her use the sword, which saved her from having to explain just where it had come from in the first place.

By the time they wanted to go over her story for the fifth time, Annja feigned exhaustion and informed them she was returning to her hotel to rest. Because she wasn't a suspect, the detectives had no choice but to let her go.

She spent the afternoon in her hotel room, catching up on email and watching the news. There was no mention of the events at the museum. Connolly probably made sure it wasn't mentioned, she thought, and for once didn't mind that someone had used their influence to kill a story.

The question of who had tried to kidnap her weighed heavily on her. The truth was that she had disrupted quite a few criminal enterprises in her role as bearer of the sword and any one of them could have decided to try to even the score. The gunman's own words seemed to suggest as much.

When evening came she took a shower and then swapped her shorts, T-shirt and boots for well-tailored pants and a cotton blouse. The cream-colored shirt complemented her tanned skin and made her green eyes stand out sharply. She surveyed herself in the mirror, decided it would have to do and caught a cab to Canela.

Apparently she'd chosen well, as she drew more than a few glances threading her way through the restaurant behind the maître d'. Connolly was already at the table, waiting. He stood when he saw her approaching and moved to hold her chair for her.

She sat, thanked him and took the menu from the waiter.

"What's good here?" she asked her host.

"Honestly? Everything," he replied. "The fish is flown in from the Mediterranean daily and the beef is grass-fed from Australia."

They exchanged small talk while waiting for dinner and then mostly ate in silence. The food was superb, everything Annja had expected it to be, and she was able to put the day's events behind her and enjoy the evening.

While they were waiting for dessert, Connolly removed an iPad from an attaché case at his feet and turned it on. Without any explanation, he placed the iPad on the table in front of her. On the screen was the image of an ancient metal scroll similar to the ones she'd been looking at that afternoon at the Shrine of the Book. In fact she thought at first she *was* looking at the Copper Scroll again. Except that the Copper Scroll had been cut into fragments to open it; this one was intact. The writing, however, appeared to also be the same Hebrew lettering.

Without looking up, she asked, "Is it copper?"

"Bronze, actually, though a tin alloy rather than an arsenic base."

That would make the metal easier to work with while at the same time eliminating the danger of working with arsenic for the metallurgist.

She picked up the iPad and brought it closer, trying to make out the Hebrew characters. She recognized a few, but unfortunately, ancient Hebrew was not one of her fortes.

"Swipe the screen to the left to see an English translation," Connolly suggested.

The translated document was laid out as the scroll had been, with two columns stretching down either side of the page, each with thirty-two separate stanzas. That similarity to the Copper Scroll didn't escape her.

Annja felt a surge of excitement. Could it be?

She looked up and caught Connolly watching her. Something about the expression on his face made her ask, "Is it real?"

He nodded. "As far as I can tell. I've had a variety of tests done on it and my people are confident it isn't a hoax. Whether the information on it is correct or not, well, that's another issue."

Annja shook her head. "That's the only issue, actually."

"Ah, so you recognize it, don't you?"

Now it was her turn to shrug. "I know what I think it is, at least. Whether you and I consider it to be the same thing remains to be seen."

Connolly laughed. "Are you always this careful with what you say?"

"Of course. Aren't you?"

"Touché, Ms. Creed, touché." He smiled wryly, paused a moment to take a sip of his drink and then went on. "I'm also a man who believes in getting to the point.

"The scroll, which I'm calling the Bronze Scroll for obvious reasons, was discovered during an excavation at Masada in 2001. It was immediately placed in a private collection and remained there until I acquired that collection last month as partial payment on a business debt."

He paused before continuing. "I'm convinced that the Bronze Scroll is the mate to the Copper Scroll at the shrine. Either one alone is useless but, together, they should lead us right to the ancient Jewish Temple's hidden caches."

"Us?" Annja asked.

"Yes, us. I would like to hire you to run the expedition for me. As I'm sure you've noticed, money is not an issue. You'll have the very best of whatever you need to get the job done."

"Why not just do it yourself?"

"Me?" Connolly asked with a laugh. "What the hell do I know about running an expedition?"

Annja had to give him credit for knowing his limits. Organizing and running an archaeological dig of this size and magnitude would be an absolute bear. An experienced hand was going to be needed to make certain they had the right people and equipment, never mind the various permits that were going to be needed. Of course, whatever they found would belong to the Israeli government, but they'd get their ten percent finder's fee, which would be more than enough given the size of the treasure they expected to find. If she started now, she could work on the details between assignments for *Chasing History's Monsters* and perhaps have everything ready for spring....

"I'll be along for the ride," Connolly added, "but you'll be in charge of the details. There is, however, one caveat."

"Which is?"

"Everything has to be ready to go within seventy-two hours."

Annja nearly choked on her wine.

Seventy-two hours? He can't be serious…

"The permits I have in place with the Israeli government will expire in three days. If that happens, I'll be forced to wait until next year before launching the expedition," Connolly told her. "Too much can happen. Knowledge of the scroll could leak to the wrong parties, another explorer might stumble upon one of the caches. Hell, the Arabs and Israelis might go to war! Those are risks I'm not willing to take. But if the effort is under way, the permit's extension clause is activated and I can stay in the field with my team an extra ninety days."

He stared intensely across the table at her. "Seventy-two hours. Not a moment longer. Can you do it?"

Annja's thoughts whirled. Connolly had said that money was no object. There shouldn't be a problem recruiting experienced hands, either, especially not once they heard she'd be able to pay them a decent wage. Hell, she'd have to beat them off with a stick.

For once, her own schedule wouldn't be a problem, either. She had a week left of her vacation time and she was sure she could swing more, especially if the information on the Bronze Scroll turned out to be correct. If that happened, she knew her producer, Doug Morrell, would give his left leg to get *Chasing History's Monsters* involved in the discovery. It was just too big an archaeological find for the show to ignore. Not even the lack of a monster associated with the legend of the Copper Scroll would slow Morrell down once he was determined to be involved. He'd just invent one if he needed to.

The events at the Shrine of the Book earlier that afternoon gave her another reason to accept the offer. Being out in the field would make it harder for her enemies, whoever they were, to track her down and would reduce the chance of innocent people being injured in the crossfire if they did. That gunman could have injured a number of bystanders and caused considerable damage to the artifacts in the shrine if he had opened up as he'd threatened to do. Laying low would help her avoid any potentially dangerous situations of a similar nature.

At least for the time being.

Decision made, she looked up at Connolly and said the words he had been waiting to hear.

"You've got yourself an expedition leader."

7

Organizing an expedition, regardless of the size, was never easy. Putting one together at the last minute was most likely next to impossible. Annja knew this and yet she was determined to meet the deadline because doing so meant she'd be able to get to work solving the mystery of the Bronze and Copper scrolls that much faster. Never mind the little issue of losing her spot on the expedition if they had to wait another season to get the permits reissued.

Before the end of their meal the previous night, Connolly had told her she was free to use office space at the local branch of Excelsior Mining and Gas (EMG) and she showed up outside their front door shortly after nine this morning, ready to get to work. The secretary had been apprised of her arrival and Annja was quickly shown to a large corner office that looked out onto the street behind the building. Anticipating that she would need some help, Connolly had also arranged for one of his senior VPs, Martin Grimes, to assist in whatever way she thought necessary.

Grimes was in his mid-thirties, a hard-looking no-nonsense individual who was intimately familiar with the breadth and scope of Connolly's vast empire and who apparently didn't know how to take no for an answer. He was there waiting for her when she arrived and didn't waste any time rolling up his sleeves and diving into the task before them.

She compiled a list of all the gear they would need to support the team in the field and to properly excavate each site. Since Grimes had direct access to the expense account Connolly had set up for the expedition, she handed the list over to him and left it in his hands to secure the items. That left her free to deal with personnel and logistics.

A fair amount of the work on the latter had already been done, she quickly discovered. The permits were quite extensive and upon seeing them she instantly understood why Connolly didn't want them to go to waste. The Israeli government had hired Connolly's mining company to survey the Negev Desert for mineral and natural gas deposits. The agreement basically gave them carte blanche to go where they wanted outside the settled regions to drill for samples. The language was written rather loosely, no doubt something Connolly had pushed for knowing what he intended to do with the permits, and would easily cover any excavation work. Anything found under the auspices of the permit had to be reported to the government, which helped the slight concern she still had that Connolly might abscond with the treasure.

Satisfied that the expedition would be operating within the bounds of the law, Annja turned her attention to rounding up some experienced hands. Connolly might see this as a hunt for buried treasure, but Annja certainly didn't. If they actually found what they were looking for, it would have considerable import as an archaeological find and she needed to make sure they properly documented and handled their finds. There were plenty of senior archaeologists she would love to have as part of the expedition, but it was unrealistic to expect them to drop whatever they were doing to join her dig on a day's notice. Which meant she was going to have to go to an entirely different well.

She picked up the phone and dialed a number from memory, which connected her to the switchboard at the Hebrew University of Jerusalem's Institute of Archaeology. When the operator answered, Annja asked to be connected to Professor Ephraim Yellin. A few moments later a gruff, male voice came on the line.

"Hello?"

"Ephraim? It's Annja."

"Annja! How good to hear from you. Has that T.V. program been keeping you busy?"

"More than I like to think about," she admitted with a self-deprecating laugh.

"Well, then you need to get back in the field. Get

your hands dirty. Archaeologists can't be away from the earth too long, you know. Makes us cranky!"

Isn't that the truth. "That's exactly why I'm calling, Ephraim. I need your help with something field-related."

"Ask away, my dear girl."

The two had met at a symposium several years ago and had become fast friends, despite the fact that Ephraim was at least thirty years her senior. She'd been planning to stop in to see him later this week. Until her dinner with Connolly the night before changed more than a few of her plans.

"I'm putting together a dig at the last minute. Just a small one, mind you, but I need extra hands to help with the field work."

"Tsk, tsk. Always in a hurry, aren't you, Annja?" he said, good-naturedly. "No matter. Tell me what you are after and I'll see if I can help."

Annja had an answer ready for him, even though she hated keeping the full truth secret. "It's nothing really, just a client with a lead on the site of a possible first-century Roman encampment. I need four, maybe five people on the ground with me to handle the client's request. Nothing fancy, basic experience will do."

"First-century Roman, huh? A little outside your usual area, isn't it?"

Annja's professional expertise was in European history. "Aren't you the one who's always telling me that change is good for the soul, Ephraim? I needed to get my hands dirty and the opportunity fell into my lap. Do you think you can help me round up extra help?"

"If you don't mind graduate students, I can probably get you half a dozen or so. When do you need them?"

"Tomorrow morning?"

It sounded as if he was choking. "A hurry is right! No matter. I'll have them by early tomorrow morning."

"Thanks. I owe you one, Ephraim."

"You owe me more than one, Annja. But don't worry, I'll just add it to your tab." Ephraim was laughing as he ended the call.

Knowing her need for warm bodies was taken care of, Annja turned her attention to scaring up the rest of the equipment they would need. She had given Grimes a list of the common supplies necessary for camp life, from tents to the many gallons of water they were no doubt going to consume under the desert sun, leaving her to procure the more dig-specific gear herself. A few calls to some friends in the field gave her the numbers of half a dozen suppliers in Jerusalem, and the fact that money wasn't an issue allowed her to have the gear delivered right to Connelly's offices starting that very afternoon. What she couldn't find directly from the suppliers she was able to beg from the antiquities departments of two of the local universities.

Grimes came back sometime in the midafternoon and dropped six sets of keys on the desk in front of her.

"What are these for?" she asked.

"Take a look out the window and see."

Annja got up, walked over to the window he was indicating and spread the slats of the blinds open with one hand. Parked outside in the lot behind the building were six Land Cruisers, outfitted for expedition work with off-road tires and roof racks brimming with equipment. Three of the six were equipped with front-mounted winches and each of them had spare tanks of gasoline in racks mounted on the rear doors.

"Wow! Terrific," she told him. "But why six? We'll have less than two people per vehicle."

"You're forgetting about Mr. Connolly's security team."

Security team? How could she forget about a security team she hadn't heard anything about yet? She said as much to Grimes.

"Sorry. Must have been an oversight. After the events at the museum the other day, I've advised Mr. Connolly not to go anywhere without a nine-man security detail. They will accompany him on the expedition, but won't interfere in any way unless something occurs to put him in danger. I've taken the liberty of expanding your supply list to accommodate the eight extras."

"Eight? I thought you said the security detail had nine men in it?"

"I'm the ninth," Grimes said with a smile that was distinctly predatory.

Annja realized that ending up on the wrong side of a confrontation with the man would most likely be unpleasant for all involved. Very unpleasant.

8

Annja arrived outside the building that housed Ephraim's office the next morning behind the wheel of one of their new expedition vehicles and found six people and a pile of gear waiting for her. She parked, got out of the truck and approached the closest, a stocky gray-haired man of about sixty.

"Well, if it isn't the famous television star herself!" Ephraim said as she drew near.

She couldn't help but match his wide smile with one of her own. "It's good to see you, too, *old* friend." She made sure to overemphasize the word *old,* then laughed with him at their habitual welcome.

She turned and surveyed the group. They were all in their early twenties, closer to Doug Morrell's age than her own, and seeing them made her flash back to England and her first major dig at Hadrian's Wall. It had been an amazing experience and she had no doubt this crew was going to remember this dig for the rest of their lives.

Especially once we tell them what we're hunting for.

There were three men and two women waiting patiently behind Ephraim, and Annja introduced herself. Benjamin Natchyu was Israeli and doing Ph.D. work on the Second Temple period of Jewish history. He'd worked with Ephraim on several of his expeditions and had the most field experience among the students. Mike Collins and Tony Green were big Midwestern boys from the University of Arkansas, where they were doing masters-level work on Paleolithic settlements and their impact on the rise of agriculture. They were currently in Jerusalem as part of an exchange program and had jumped at the chance to get out of the classroom and participate in an actual dig.

"Wow!" Tony said when Annja introduced herself. "You're even more beautiful in person than you are on television." He immediately flushed bright red, which of course ruined the suave, man-of-the-world persona he was trying to project. That made Annja like him all the more.

"Ignore the big guy over there," one of the two women said good-naturedly. "He tries hard but I don't think he'd know what to do with himself if you or any other woman responded to his come-ons."

Mike roared with laughter and slapped Tony on the back. Tony flushed even brighter if that was at all possible and shot the tall blonde the finger, smiling all the while. Annja decided that she might just like this little group.

The woman who'd spoken turned out to be Susan Hollister. A lithe blonde with pale blue eyes and an athlete's physique. She hailed from London, spoke with a clipped British accent and had come to Jerusalem specifically to study with Professor Yellin.

Her friend, Rachel Golan, was a good four inches shorter, with a figure that could best be called plump and long dark hair the color of mud. Like Benjamin, she was a native Israeli, but had fallen into archaeology and wasn't sure yet if she intended to dedicate her life to it. When Hollister announced she was volunteering to join the group, Golan had quickly followed suit.

"All right, children," Ephraim finally said, "settle down. I'm sure Annja has more to do today than listen to the lot of you trade insults. Let's get the gear packed up and be on our way."

Annja turned and looked at him. "Our way?" she asked.

He nodded, then waved her over. "Yes, our way," he said quietly when she was close enough. "You're up to something, I know it, and it's not just some first-century Roman household you're investigating, now is it?"

She feigned a look of surprise. "Would I keep you in the dark like that, my friend?"

"Yes, you would. You can't fool my nose for intrigue, Annja Creed. When was the last time you worked an expedition, or did anything for that matter, without extensive planning? You're up to something, and when you're up to something that usually means the rest of us are going to miss out on an amazing find. Not this time, I tell you, not this time. I'm going with you."

Annja laughed. She couldn't fault him for his reasoning, which was, after all, correct. It would be a huge advantage to have him along. His knowledge of early Jewish history was practically encyclopedic.

"All right, all right, you win! Welcome aboard."

Grinning like the Cheshire cat, Ephraim moved to help the others load the rest of the gear into the back of the truck.

AFTER ARRIVING BACK at the EMG office Annja had been using as base camp, she put the graduate students to work organizing, packing and then reloading the gear. While they were doing that, Annja took Ephraim into her office to bring him up to speed.

She explained how the expedition was being sponsored by Mitchell Connolly, which Ephraim had already guessed given they were currently sitting in the man's offices. She went on to tell him about the way Connolly had come into possession of the Bronze Scroll and what they hoped to do with it. When she was finished, she sat back and waited.

"Annja," he finally said, "you realize what this could mean for the Jewish people, don't you?"

She nodded. The Temple Mount had always been the center of Jewish faith. When the Romans had destroyed it for the second time at the end of the Second Jewish Revolt in 70 CE, they had done everything they could to wipe all trace of it off the face of the planet. Only the lower edges of the western wall of the temple complex still remained today, known the world over as the Wailing Wall. It had been the site of Jewish pilgrimages for centuries. Should the paired scrolls, Bronze and Copper, lead them to the temple's storied riches the way they expected them to, and should those riches be confirmed as having come from the temple complex in the months just before its destruction, they would have an immeasurable impact on Israel. Not to mention the Jewish faith across the world.

It was a daunting prospect.

"You are aware of the legend of the guardians, yes?" Ephraim asked.

Annja shook her head.

Ephraim took a moment to gather his thoughts, then told her what he knew. "Legends say that the high priests in the temple knew Titus was going to order its destruction. Some say the message came from spies within the Roman legions, others that it was a direct warning from God. In either case, the high priests acted on that warning, removing the treasure from the inner sanctum and arranging to have it split up and hidden in the countryside to keep it out of Roman hands.

"A group of warriors known as the Gibborim, or the Mightiest, were ordered to keep the treasure safe until it could be restored to its rightful place. Legend has it that the Gibborim were directly descended from the Mighty Men of King David's reign."

Annja thought about that for a moment. "But they wouldn't have been able to carry out their orders, since the Romans destroyed the temple to put an end to the revolt."

"Correct," Ephraim replied. "Which is why there are those who say that the Gibborim are still out there, guarding the treasure, passing down their responsibility through the generations until the temple is restored and the Jewish riches can be returned to the Holiest of Holies."

It sounded outlandish, but Annja knew legends often had a kernel of truth in them. And then there was the strange, bearded man who had confronted her in the museum two days before. Could he have been an agent of the Gibborim?

Don't be an idiot, Annja. It's just a legend.

Except in Annja's world, legends had a way of coming to life on far too regular a basis.

"We'll worry about the Gibborim if and when we find the treasure," she said. "In order to do that, we have to pick a place to start looking."

That was actually the most critical and most difficult task facing them. Late last night Annja had paired the verses from the Bronze Scroll with those from the Copper Scroll. She had assumed a direct one-to-one ratio—the first verse from the Bronze Scroll was paired with the first verse from the Copper Scroll. The stanzas seemed to fit together that way, or at least there weren't any obvious inconsistencies. For all she knew, the writer had tried to conceal the connection between the two documents by pairing them in reverse order or some other more obscure method. The recipients had no doubt known the correct process, but Annja had nothing more to go on than the syntax of the stanzas themselves. If the writer had been clever with the layout, they were going to have to find out in the field the hard way.

Now that the pairings were done, it was up to Annja and Ephraim to look them over and choose the ones they thought had the best chance of success. Finding even one of the hidden caches would tell them that their methods were correct and would make it immeasurably easier to find the others.

They settled in to examine the possibilities and quickly found that even with the help of the information from the Bronze Scroll, the directions to the alleged treasure sites from the Copper Scroll where difficult to decipher. They were filled with references to what the writer no doubt thought would be obvious landmarks. For the most part those references had long since passed out of popular knowledge.

The two of them poured over the paired stanzas, looking for one in which the references were recognizable to the old Jewish archaeologist. Thankfully it didn't take long. Ephraim's eyes lit up when he spotted the seventh pairing.

"Listen," he said, and then read the verses aloud to her. "'From the synagogue of the city in the strongholds where David dwelt, travel one day's march to the home of the tax collector. In the great cistern of the courtyard of the peristyle, in a hollow in the floor covered with sediment, in front of the upper opening: ninety talents.'"

Annja knew the first sentence had come from the Bronze Scroll, which gave them their starting point. The David referenced in the verse had to be King David, one of the ancient rulers of Israel and a major figure in the Old Testament. She did not, however, have any idea what city the verse was referring to nor where David's strongholds might be found.

From the look on his face, however, Ephraim did.

"It is a reference to the twenty-third verse of the First Book of Samuel," he told her excitedly. He quoted, "'And David went up from hence and dwelt in the strongholds of Engedi.'"

"And you know where, and what, this Engedi is?"

Ephraim nodded. "Yes, yes, Annja! Ein Gedi is both the name of an oasis and the town that was built alongside it. It is about fifty kilometers south of Jerusalem, not far from the shores of the Dead Sea."

"Was there a synagogue there?" Annja asked, and then realized what a ridiculous question it was. Any good-size Jewish city from that time period had a synagogue. The question she should have asked was whether or not they had any information about where the synagogue had been built. Knowing where the city had been was all well and good, but if they couldn't find the location of the synagogue they might as well throw darts to determine which direction they needed to travel.

"The ruins of the city are open to the public, as is the synagogue itself. It has the most beautiful stone mosaic floor, something you will not want to miss, I assure you. We can use that as our starting point and travel north until we find the ruins of the tax collector's house. If ruins still exist."

Right, she thought. If.

Still, she'd found archaeological sites on a lot less.

Tomorrow it would begin.

9

The morning of the third day after the meeting in the restaurant, the last day of the seventy-two-hour deadline, dawned bright and clear. The team rose early and was ready to go by the time Connolly and his security team showed up just before nine.

Grimes introduced Annja to each of the men. Annja did her best to remember their names—Hamilton, Gardner, Chan, the guy with the scar on his chin, the one with the nose that was broken that hadn't healed properly—but eventually gave up. She'd learn the names along the way and that was that.

They were all cut from the same cloth, it seemed—hard, rugged men between the ages of twenty and thirty, most with former military experience. They were polite, but didn't say much, and Annja knew they would do their jobs and that was all. She doubted very much she was going to be getting any of them to sling shovelfuls of dirt. As long as they stayed out of her excavation.

Annja and Grimes put their heads together for a

few minutes and got everyone assigned to the appropriate vehicles. Annja, Grimes and Connolly would take the lead. Immediately behind, two trucks would carry three security team members and their gear. The fourth truck would be driven by Tony and carry Rachel and Ephraim. Susan, Mike and Benjamin would be in the fifth vehicle, with the final two security team members bringing up the rear in the sixth, and last.

Their first destination was Tel Goren, a low hill just north of the western shore of the Dead Sea and about sixty miles southwest of Jerusalem. This was the site of the original village known as Engedi, a small village destroyed by the Assyrians around 600 BCE. From there they would move slightly northeast, up along a nearby ridgeline to where the Jewish village of the same name had thrived during the Roman occupation of Israel. Internet research Annja had done the night before told her that the place had been large, about forty acres, and prosperous from the date and perfume trade. As Ephraim had explained, the remains of the synagogue mentioned in the scroll still stood today and it was from that point that they would begin their search for the house of the tax collector.

If they could find that, they should be able to find the ninety talents.

Or so she hoped.

Neither Grimes nor Connolly appeared to be in the mood for conversation, so Annja kept to herself as they made the hour and a half drive south from Jerusalem.

The countryside reminded her of the time she'd spent at a dig in Iraq. There was the same rugged landscape, the same drab coloration. Occasionally they would pass an oasis where the bright green of the vegetation would break up the monotony of the rest of the countryside, but it didn't last long.

By midmorning they reached Tel Goren and made the short drive up the ridgeline to the site of the ruins of Engedi. Most of the structures were nothing more than knee-high stone walls after all this time, but even so Annja and the others were able to see how the town had been laid out for maximum use of the space available.

The synagogue was easy to find because it was the only building over which a permanent tentlike structure had been erected. To protect it from the elements. They parked as close as they were able and then got out. Annja waved Ephraim over to where she stood with Grimes and Connolly.

"All right, Annja, it's your show. What's next?" Connolly asked.

Annja quoted from the scroll. "'From the synagogue of the city in the stronghold where David dwelt, travel one day's march to the home of the tax collector.'"

"One day's travel?" Grimes repeated. "What's that? Ten, maybe fifteen miles at best over rugged ground like this?"

Ephraim shook his head. "It says one day's march, which means it is actually a measurement equal to the distance that a Roman legion could march in a typical five-hour period."

Annja had learned a fair degree about Roman culture during her work on Hadrian's Wall. "Twenty miles," she told them. "A fully equipped Roman legionnaire was required to march twenty miles a day."

The older archaeologist nodded. "Right. The Romans were rather exact, too, so when they said twenty miles, they meant twenty miles. We should be able to measure that with the truck's odometer and be pretty damn close to accurate. If there's anything left to find, we should be right on top of it at that point."

Grimes frowned, then waved his hands at the ancient village around them. "But how do we know which direction? Roads lead in every direction from this place."

Annja smiled. Grimes might be one hell of an executive, but when it came to ancient history, he was a babe in the woods.

"The door to the synagogue always points in the same direction—back toward Jerusalem, back toward the Holy of Holies, that place within the temple where the Spirit of the Lord dwelt," Ephraim replied. "Since the scroll mentions the synagogue as the starting place, any Jewish citizen of the time period would have known to travel in the same direction the synagogue faces. In this case, north."

They climbed back into their vehicles and began the drive north. There were no roads leading in this direction and so they were forced to drive slowly, taking care to maneuver around outcroppings of rock and ravines large enough to swallow the vehicle whole.

Just about an hour after they'd started, Grimes quietly announced, "Coming up on nineteen miles."

"Okay, pull over," Annja told him.

When he'd done so, they got out of the vehicle and waited for the others to join them.

"From this point forward we go on foot," Annja said. "I want us to form a picket line, five yards apart. Do your best to maintain that distance as we move forward. After two millennia, I'm not expecting there to be much left of the structure we're searching for, so keep your eyes peeled for any signs of permanent habitation— worked or fire-blackened stone, unusually leveled land, artifacts of any kind. Everyone with me?"

There was a chorus of affirmatives. The team was excited, which was good to see, and even Connolly and his security team were lining up, eager to take part in the search.

"If you find something, I want you to call out and then stop moving. Don't move to investigate. Just stand right where you are. Everyone else will stop at that point and maintain their positions while Ephraim and I walk over to take a look. We don't want to lose our place in the search if it turns out to be nothing, understood?"

Again a chorus of replies and more than a handful of nodding heads. Satisfied, Annja raised her arm and gave the signal for everyone to start moving forward.

If it is out there, she thought, we'll find it.

They had only walked a few hundred yards before Mike let out a shout from somewhere off to Annja's right.

"All right," she called to those immediately around her, "remember what I said. Stay in line until we're sure we need you. I'll let you know what's up as soon as I can."

When she and Ephraim reached Mike's position, she knew right away he'd hit pay dirt. A low hill stood nearby, a grove of olive trees growing in its shade. Only a few feet from the olive trees, knee-high walls of fitted stone could clearly be seen, even from a distance.

"This is it, Annja," Ephraim said. "I can feel it in my bones."

That sense of anticipation just before a major find coursed through her as she stared at what was left of a house that had stood there on that spot for more than two thousand years. Slowly, a grin spread across her face.

WITH EPHRAIM'S KNOWLEDGE of early Jewish architecture, they were able to determine the probable layout of the house from the remains that were still aboveground. From that point it didn't take them long to figure out where the peristyle, or outdoor courtyard, would have stood.

Grimes wanted to grab a shovel and start digging, but Annja would have none of that. They had hired her to conduct this expedition properly and she was going to do just that. If they did find something, she didn't want the discovery of the year sullied by complaints of improper techniques and lawsuits for potential damage to historical and cultural artifacts.

She first laid a grid over the area, using wooden stakes and long pieces of twine to divide the space into roughly even squares. Next she had Ephraim take pictures of the entire grid, documenting what every square looked like before they began. That way they could create a photo panorama of the entire site. When that was done, she divided the squares among the graduate students, giving a set to Tony and Mike, a set to Susan and Rachel and the final section to Ephraim and herself. Benjamin was tasked with documenting as much of the dig as he could with a pair of Nikon digital cameras, each with a different lens.

Two hours later they had cleared enough of the surface sand and earth to locate the remains of the cistern midway along what would have been the forward wall of the peristyle. Rectangular in shape, it reminded Annja of an oversize horse trough more than anything else. Only the floor and the slightest lip of walls remained, but it was enough for them to recognize what it was. Cheers went up from the group at the discovery.

Annja made sure Benjamin documented it with the cameras. She was getting ready to start hunting for the hollow mentioned in the scroll when Grimes walked toward her, a commercial-grade metal detector in his hand.

Annja quickly intercepted him. "What do you think you're going to do with that?" She grabbed his elbow to keep him from stepping foot inside her work area.

"What do you think?" he answered. "I'm going to save us all a bunch of time and tell you where to look."

"But…" Annja stopped. She had planned to start the search with the pulse-induction metal detectors that were a standard tool of the archaeology trade.

She stared at him, honestly stumped. All her career she'd been digging for purely archaeological reasons. To learn about a people or a culture, to verify an ancient legend, to restore a forgotten wonder to the annals of living history. Never had she conducted a dig for the sole purpose of searching for treasure. Especially not buried treasure. The very idea of using an over-the-counter metal detector hadn't even occurred to her.

"But what?" Grimes pressed.

"Nothing." She looked up and smiled at him. "Nothing at all. Excellent idea. Please, be my guest."

She got out of the way, giving him room to work. She made sure Benjamin was still taking photos with the camera and then turned back to watch.

Grimes put on the device's headphones, fiddled with the settings on the control panel and then flipped the switch. He waved the round sensor, the loop, over the ground in front of him for a moment, getting an ambient reading so he'd be able to tell what was normal background and what was not. Then he moved to where the cistern had once stood and began to move the metal detector in small circles about an inch or so above what had once been the bottom of the tank. He went back and forth from one end of the cistern to the other, methodically covering the entire area. When he was finished, he turned off the metal detector, took off the headphones and turned to them, a big smile on his face. He pointed to the back corner.

"Right there," he said. "Dig right there."

They found the first treasure cache less then fifteen minutes later.

10

They set up camp near the end of the afternoon close to the ruins. The trucks were arranged in a semicircular pattern with their noses pointed outward. A fire pit was dug in the center of the area just behind them and the tents set up on the other side of the pit, the ruins at their backs. Connolly shared a large canvas safari tent with Grimes, while the security team members were paired up in standard issue two-man army field tents. Both Anna and Ephraim had their own tents, while the male graduate students shared one and the female graduate students shared another.

After dinner that night, Annja and the others celebrated their find, ecstatic that their efforts had paid off so early in the expedition. It had truly been a spectacular find. The gold had been buried in a set of earthen jars, sealed with wax and stacked one on top of the other. Over time some of the jars had cracked, spilling gold over the rest of the pile.

A talent was a measure of weight equal to about sixty

kilograms, which meant by the time they were finished extracting the jars they had over five thousands kilograms of gold sitting in front of them. At current market prices, a single talent was worth about $840,000. That meant their entire haul, from just the first of sixty-four different treasure caches, equaled somewhere in the neighborhood of seventy-five million dollars.

Seventy-five million. Annja could barely believe it.

They couldn't keep it, of course. Arguments would be made that it was part of the Israeli national heritage and Annja agreed with that. But the ten percent finder's fee, split seventeen ways, meant each of them was walking away with almost five hundred thousand dollars from this one site alone.

That was worth partying over.

Discovering that Ben was a fan of American rock from the 1980s and that he had an iPod full of tunes with him, Mike jury-rigged a connection to the sound system in one of the Land Cruisers and after dinner that night the desert air was filled with the sound of Eddie Van Halen on the guitar and David Lee Roth singing about California girls and the summer sun. It wasn't long before Susan and Rachel were on their feet, pulling Ben and Mike with them, and gyrating to the music in the light of the campfire. Cheered on by the security team. The young people gestured for Annja to join them and at last she threw caution to the winds. It had been too long since she'd danced and she let herself go with the music.

One song led into another and another. The volume was cranked higher every time someone heard a song they liked. Once, Grimes came out of the tent he shared with Connolly and for a moment Annja had thought he was going to order them to turn it off and go to bed, like a parent with wayward teenagers partying too long. But he simply watched them for a moment and disappeared back inside.

Guy needs to learn how to relax.

Less than a minute later a sudden, heavy sense of impending doom overtook her, like a thousand ghosts drifting across her own grave, and she faltered, then stopped dancing altogether.

She glanced around. Ever since taking up the sword she seemed to have a heightened sense of danger and she'd learned to trust that feeling for what it was, an early alarm system. And right now it was blaring away like an air raid siren in the middle of a blitz.

The celebration continued without her. Her companions danced or lounged around the fire, talking and laughing. The music rose up into the night, the guitar wailing, the drumbeat pounding out a rhythm....

A rhythm that sounded familiar.

Like the beat of horses' hooves.

Annja spun around, fully expecting to see a horde of horsemen thundering toward them.

But there was no one there.

The night was as dark and as empty as it had been just moments before.

Her senses were still on full alert and she knew they were no longer alone. She might not be able to see anyone yet, but she was positive they were out there, somewhere.

She walked over to the iPod and cut the music off abruptly, eliciting a round of cries from the others.

"What do you think you're doing, Annja?"

"Turn that back on!"

"Hey! I liked that song."

She held up her hand for silence as she turned in a slow circle, looking out beyond the campfire into the night.

Suddenly Grimes was there by her side, a pistol in his hand.

The sight of the gun shocked those still complaining into silence.

"What is it?" Grimes asked, his own gaze now turned outward, the pistol held barrel down in his right hand, ready to be brought up at a moment's notice.

"I'm not sure. I feel like—"

"There's something out there," he finished for her. She nodded.

Grimes opened his mouth to say something else but he was cut off as the deep mournful sound of a horn split the night air.

Baaaaawhoooooooooooooooooooooooo.

Everyone froze. As if the sound had stunned them into immobility. It was only when the sound began to fade away that they turned and looked at one another.

"What the hell was that?" someone asked, and Annja found herself wondering the same thing.

What *was* that? And, more importantly, where was it coming from?

The horn sounded again, the same deep, sonorous bellow that went on and on.

Except this time it was answered, answered from several different directions at the same time.

Whoever they are, they have us surrounded.

The thought must have occurred to Grimes at the same time. He instantly began shouting orders at the men around him.

"Move, move! I want a secure perimeter around Mr. Connolly's tent ten seconds ago! Four-foot intervals, ten feet out from the center. Try not to shoot the civilians."

Annja didn't know if that last was meant as a joke or not, but she wasn't going to take any chances. She rounded up Ephraim and the students and hustled them inside one of the other tents, out of the security team's line of fire. The last thing they needed was to have one of them mistaken for an intruder. Tensions were high as the security team swiftly moved to create a defensive cordon around their employer and the millions of dollars in gold inside his tent.

"What's going on?" Rachel asked as Annja hurried her along with a hand on her arm.

"I'm not sure, but the security team has it under control. You just get under cover, all right?"

Annja looked over her shoulder and caught Ephraim's

stare. He mouthed a single word—*Gibborim*—and then turned away to calm the students.

Annja took up a position just outside the tent door, her hands loose and hanging at her sides, ready for action no matter what happened. Her fingers twitched and for a split second she had the sword in her hand before she banished it back to the otherwhere. She didn't want it until she needed it. Too many explanations to make otherwise.

The horn rang out twice more and each time it was answered by a chorus of others, though never from the same place twice. Annja had the sense that the enemy was moving in a slow circle around them so they couldn't pinpoint their exact locations. Truth was, it wasn't a bad strategy.

Then, just like that, the horns stopped.

Silence settled back over the night like a wet cloak.

She was peering into the darkness, trying to spot whoever might be out there.

"It's a call to battle."

Annja jumped. She turned to find Ephraim standing at her elbow, concerned as he looked out into the night.

"Jeez, you scared me!"

Ephraim had the decency to appear embarrassed. "Sorry," he said.

After her heart had calmed enough for her to breathe more easily, she said, "A call to battle?"

The old Israeli inclined his head toward the surrounding darkness. "The sound of the shofar calls the warriors to battle. It will not be heard again until the battle is over."

It took Annja a moment to make the mental connection between the long, twisting instrument made from a sheep's horn, an instrument known as the shofar, with the braying sound they'd been hearing for the past ten minutes. Once she did she was amazed she hadn't immediately recognized it. She'd heard a shofar played at a concert in New York a few years ago and the noise it produced was quite distinctive.

"Who's playing it?"

Ephraim didn't look at her as he said, "You know who."

"The Gibborim?"

The older man nodded.

"You don't believe that."

He turned to her. "I don't?"

"No, you don't," she told him, "and neither do I. Let's forget for a minute that it has been two thousand years since the treasure was hidden and that it is damned near impossible to get people to stick with a task for five minutes these days, never mind for two millennia. Let's just consider the sheer scale of the task. How would a small group of men watch over sixty-four different treasure sites scattered across the country?"

Ephraim didn't say anything.

"How many men would you need to do that effectively? Every day, every night, year after year? How would you hide them in today's day and age, when a satellite the size of a toaster can see a rock the size of my thumbnail with absolute accuracy?" She shook her head. "We would have seen them by now, Ephraim."

But her logic didn't sway him. "The Lord works in mysterious ways, Annja, and His people are watching us right now to see how we handle the temple treasure. How else would you explain someone's appearance so soon after we removed the gold?"

It was dark and in the shadows Annja couldn't see if he was teasing her or not. She didn't want to offend him but she had become an archaeologist so she could look at the history beneath the myth and legend.

In a careful tone, she said, "I could explain it half a dozen ways, Ephraim, but the most likely is that they are locals trying to scare us off in the hopes we'll leave behind whatever we've found. So they can claim it for themselves."

Leave behind nearly a million dollars in ancient gold coins? Not bloody likely.

It seemed that whoever they had been, members of the ancient Gibborim sect or desert dwellers looking for an easy score, they were gone now.

As Grimes ordered his men to stand down and began to set up a watch schedule to get them through morning, Annja let the others know that the crisis had passed. Not surprisingly, no one wanted to return to their festivities, so good nights were exchanged and the group headed off to their respective tents.

Annja washed up, undressed, then pulled on the

T-shirt and sweats she wore as pajamas in the field. She slipped into her sleeping bag and doused the camp light. But as she lay there, her thoughts kept drifting back to the sound of the horns in the night and the explanation Ephraim had given for them.

A call to battle.

But a battle for what?

And against whom?

Sleep was a long time coming.

11

"I'm telling you, she had a sword. The same freakin' sword she had in the museum. It was there one second and gone the next."

Connolly stared at his second-in-command and wondered if the desert sun was starting to get to him.

"What do you mean it was gone?" he asked. "Did she put it down?"

"No. If I hadn't seen it with my own eyes I wouldn't have believed it, but I'm telling you that the sword appeared out of nowhere and then vanished just like that!" He snapped his fingers.

Very carefully, Connolly said, "So you're telling me that she made a sword, a medieval broadsword no less, appear out of thin air and then vanish again in the blink of an eye?"

Grimes nodded. "Yes, that's what I'm telling you."

"Hardly sounds possible, does it?"

The other man grunted. "I know what it sounds like, Mitchell. I know it sounds absolutely crazy. But I saw it. Not once, but twice. First in the museum and now here. There's something strange about that woman."

Connolly had known that since the moment he'd first met her. Not only was she strikingly beautiful, she was also extremely capable. And yet…

And yet there was something in her, something lurking just beneath the surface.

The Creed woman made him uneasy and he always felt like he was under intense scrutiny whenever she was close.

There was definitely more to Annja Creed than first met the eye.

Grimes was looking at him with one of those "am I crazy" expressions and Connolly waved impatiently.

"Relax," he told him. "I trust you. If you say you saw it, then you saw it. I'll take your word for it. We both know there are weirder things than a sword that appears and disappears."

And wasn't that the truth. All you had to do was look at why they were out here to understand that.

He didn't care about the gold. What the hell was he going to do with a few more million dollars? That was petty cash, for heaven's sake.

No, he had an entirely different reason for seeking out the various treasure caches. A few odds and ends had been hidden away with the coins and he was looking for one in particular.

A staff. A very special staff.

One that, in the hands of a young man named Aaron,

had been used to perform some amazing feats of power and might.

Connolly aimed to make that staff his own.

That was what this expedition was for, after all.

Money would only get you so far. He should know; he had more than he could ever spend, never mind need. But with the staff…the man who held the staff could rule the world.

"I want her and the old man to translate the twenty-seventh stanza in the morning. Wherever it tells us to go, that's where we're headed."

Grimes winced. "I'm not so sure that's a good idea, Mitchell."

"And why's that?" he asked impatiently.

The other man didn't back down. "We're not ready, that's why. We've only tested one of their interpretations of the stanzas. They might have gotten lucky and, if so, we'd be off on some wild-goose chase. That's what we hired her to avoid, remember?"

Connolly nodded and, seeing it, Grimes went on.

"We should try again. Sure, we can get them to translate the staff stanza, but we'll get them to work on a couple at the same time. Not let them know the significance of the treasure in Stanza 27. Then follow another trail. At least once, maybe twice, even three times. The staff isn't going anywhere, boss. It's been there, wherever *there* is, for thousands of years. It isn't suddenly going to sprout legs and walk away. We can afford to do this right. When we're certain their methods work, we'll get them to give us the location and then we'll get rid of them once and for all."

As much as he didn't want to admit it, Grimes was right. They shouldn't rush. Do it right the first time, his father had always told him as a boy, and you won't have to do it again. He'd created his fortune by only doing things once.

A troubling thought reared its head.

"What about these Gibborim, or whatever the hell they are called?"

"You leave the locals—or whoever those guys were—to me. If they ever decide to show their faces, we'll blow their heads off their shoulders from four hundred yards away. Introduce them to modern weaponry the old-fashioned way."

With that, Connolly was satisfied.

12

The rest of the night passed without incident. Annja didn't fall asleep until well past midnight and when she did it was a restless, uneasy sleep. She dreamed of the desert and of fire and awoke in the morning feeling less rested than when she'd gone to bed.

Not a good start for the day.

She joined the others for breakfast around the campfire, discovering in the process that Ephraim was a good cook. He managed to make powdered eggs and oatmeal actually taste good, sending her back for seconds.

They were just cleaning up when they heard the unmistakable sound of an approaching helicopter. Rachel saw it first, pointing it out to the others as it came in from the north, the white EMG logo clearly visible on the black fuselage. Annja was glad they'd finished breakfast. A gritty breeze washed over them as the helicopter touched down a few dozen yards outside of camp.

The helicopter was carrying padded lockboxes in which to secure the jars of gold coins that the team had unearthed the day before. Each box would be carefully labeled, locked, loaded onto the chopper and then flown to a secure holding facility where it would eventually be examined by representatives from Israel's Department of Antiquities.

The idea of driving around the Israeli countryside with millions of dollars worth of gold in the back of their trucks just wasn't smart. Even a second-grader would have known that. They just didn't have the equipment or the manpower to protect it properly. If word got out about what they were carrying, they would become a big, fat target. The gold would be very easy to move on the black market once it had been melted down.

The two-way radio on her belt beeped and she answered it. Grimes.

"What's up?" she asked.

"Mitchell would like a word, if you have a moment."

"Of course, I'll be right there."

She replaced the radio and then headed across camp to where Connolly's safari-style canvas tent had been erected the night before. She found Grimes waiting for her at the entrance and followed him inside.

Unlike her own tent, which was a portable nylon backpacking tent designed to be light and easy to use, Connolly's home-away-from-home had been designed for comfort. It had a wooden floor, two cots, several folding chairs and even a portable sink in one corner. Connolly was standing in front of the sink, shaving with a straight razor, when Annja entered.

"Ah, just the person I was looking for," he said good-naturedly, as if her appearance was a surprise and he hadn't just asked Grimes to call her.

"Morning to you, as well," she replied.

"Please, sit." He pointed at one of the folding camp chairs with his razor.

Connolly finished up, wiped his face with a towel and came over to sit next to her.

"Coffee?" he asked.

"Cocoa, if you have it…"

"Certainly. Grimes?"

They sat in silence until Grimes brought their drinks and joined them, a cup of coffee of his own in hand. Connolly didn't waste any time getting down to business.

"Do you have any idea who or what that was last night?"

"No, I don't."

"Want to hazard a guess?"

Annja shrugged. "Some of the locals, probably. My guess is they think we're here to do a prolonged excavation and those have a tendency to close down a site, turning away tourist dollars."

Grimes frowned. "I can't imagine this place getting many tourists."

"My point exactly," Annja replied.

"Do you think it could be one of those—what did Ephraim call them earlier—Grig-something-or-others?"

"Gibborim," she corrected almost automatically.

Connolly had already proved he had a penchant for unusual artifacts, as the ossuary box she'd sold him demonstrated, so he would no doubt have followed the stories around the Copper Scroll and its treasure pretty closely.

No sense beating around the bush.

"No, I don't think so. In fact, I don't think the Gibborim, or guardians, are anything more than an old wives' tale."

"But you've proved in the past that sometimes there is more to an old wives' tale than we think."

That was certainly true. As the "serious" host of *Chasing History's Monsters,* it was her role to debunk the legends and stories that the show investigated. Sometimes, in the process, she discovered there was a kernel of truth behind the claims.

"True. But this one seems more far-fetched than usual. The idea that a handpicked group has existed for the past two thousand years for no greater purpose than to guard some long-lost treasure seems a stretch, even for me." She shook her head. "It's going to take more than just an encounter with a desert dweller like the one we ran into last night to convince me that the Gibborim exist."

Even if Ephraim believes in them.

The two men seemed satisfied and left it at that.

"All right," Connolly said, "what's our next target?"

"Stanza 10. Ben Baraket. It's the site of an ancient Hebrew trading post from before the Roman occupation. It's located deep in the southern Negev, about thirty miles south of Mizpe Ramon."

"Mizpe Ramon?" he asked, fighting with the unfamiliar pronunciation of the word.

She nodded. "It's one of the southern development towns built in the 1950s to house Jewish refugees." She remembered all the barren space on the map she'd looked at earlier that morning, knowing she'd have to answer questions about their next site. "We can take Route 40 most of the way into Mizpe Ramon, but after that we're going to have to go overland, through some pretty treacherous terrain. I suggest we travel single file and use the two-ways to stay in touch as we go."

Grimes looked to Connolly, didn't get any objection and then nodded his head. "Agreed. We'll use the same order of travel we used yesterday and I'll have the team in the rear keep their eyes open for anyone traveling too closely to us. Just in case that old wives' tale turns out to be true."

"Fair enough," Annja replied with a laugh. "Fair enough."

KNOWING THEY HAD a good deal of distance to travel over difficult terrain, they broke camp as soon as the helicopter left and set out across the desert. Annja was in the passenger seat of the lead vehicle, constantly checking their course and direction against the notes on the iPad in her lap. Given the preciseness of the deciphered directions, even a small mistake at this juncture could send them way off track. She didn't want to have to explain to Connolly that she'd led them miles in the wrong direction. Grimes sat beside her, his gaze fixed on the road ahead. As with the day before, there wasn't much conversation.

That was why Connolly's voice startled her when he spoke up a few hours later.

"What *is* that?" he asked absently, leaning forward to get a better look out the rear window.

They had passed the small town of Mizpe Ramon a little over an hour ago and had struck out across the open desert in a western direction. There were no roads here and they were relying on Annja's sense of direction, Grimes's skill behind the wheel and their state-of-the-art GPS unit to keep them on course. This deep in the Negev there wasn't much to see except rocks and sand so Annja turned to look with real curiosity.

"What?" she asked. "Is there a problem with—"

She never finished her sentence. She'd seen the long dark line at the edge of the horizon that had caught Connolly's attention and she froze at the sight. Unlike her employer, she knew what she was looking at.

Without taking her gaze off the phenomena, she picked up the two-way radio from the seat next to her and keyed the switch.

"Rover One to Rover Five, do you copy, Benjamin?"

The young archaeologist replied, "I copy, Annja. What's up?"

"Take a look behind you and tell me that's not what I think it is."

Connolly was looking at her quizzically now and moved to say something, but she shushed him with an upright hand and a brief shake of her head. If she was right, they didn't have much time....

The radio in her hand crackled as Benjamin hit the transmit button. He shouted something in Hebrew and then, realizing that he's spoken in his native tongue, switched to English.

"It's a haboob all right, Annja! Moving fast and headed right for us!"

Annja cursed. Shoving the iPad at Connolly, who took it in bewilderment, she snatched up the topographical map from the dashboard and began scanning it frantically.

"What the hell is a haboob?" he asked with more than a hint of exasperation.

It was Grimes who answered him. "A sandstorm. A big one at that."

"That storm out there," she added, "is a monster."

"Can't we outrun it?" Connolly asked, sitting upright.

Annja shook her head. "I'm guessing that storm front is three, maybe four miles wide and it's probably moving at sixty or seventy miles per hour. These Land Cruisers are fast, sure, but there's no way we can match those speeds, not loaded down as we are. And certainly not over this kind of terrain."

"So what do we do?" Grimes asked as his gaze flicked to the rearview mirror.

A backward glance of her own confirmed her fears. The storm was gaining on them quickly. It had already gone from being a thin dark line out at the edge of the horizon to a horizontal wave of darkness moving inexorably in their direction. Even from this distance she thought she could make out the roiling eddies of sand at its forefront.

"We hope we can find a place to hole up until the storm passes."

13

The map in her hand wasn't as detailed as she would have liked, but it would have to do. She located where they had camped the night before, then estimated how much ground they had covered that morning, which would put them right about…here. She put her finger on the map in that spot and then scanned around it, looking for anything that might serve as shelter from the storm.

"Turn right," she said.

"What?" Grimes's attention was caught by whatever he was seeing in the rearview mirror.

Annja didn't hesitate, just reached over and yanked the wheel to the right. "I said turn!" she yelled.

The sudden change in direction, never mind her shout, focused his attention again. He steadied the vehicle on its new course and gripped the wheel tighter. "Where am I going?" he asked.

"There's a ridgeline on the other side of those low hills," she said, pointing to the two-story mounds of sand directly ahead of them. "Get to the other side and start looking for a place we can hole up out of the wind."

"Got it!"

As Grimes bent to the task of getting them over the shifting sands, Annja looked back again. What she saw wasn't good. The sky all around them was a sickly orange color and the storm could clearly be seen now, a veritable wall of dirt and sand hundreds of feet high churning toward them. She'd read somewhere once that haboobs could reach heights of three thousand feet and could stretch several miles across. From what she was seeing now, she guessed this one was even bigger, a great-granddaddy of a storm come to claim them.

They had to find shelter.

She picked up the two-way and spoke into it again. "Rover One to all units. There's no way we can outrun this storm, so stick close while we try to find a place to hole up and wait it out."

A chorus of "Rogers" came back to her. Satisfied, she put the radio down and turned her attention to the landscape outside the vehicle.

Grimes steered carefully down off the hill, winding his way between various rock formations and trying to keep the vehicle from tipping as the tires slid in the loose soil. Once on flat ground he headed for the wadi, or valley, between the two ridgelines ahead of them. The wind had picked up considerably in just the past few minutes, rocking the vehicle on its axles. The air was full of blowing dust and sand, limiting visibility and making it difficult for any of them to see what lay ahead. Annja had her face pressed to the glass on the passenger's side, scanning the cliff face beside them for anything that might offer safety. Connolly did the same on the other side of the vehicle.

"There!" she cried, pointing ahead of them on her side of the wadi.

Connolly slid over to her side of the vehicle, peering out the passenger window. "What is it?" he asked, trying to see through the rapidly growing murkiness.

Annja pointed to a dark shadow on the cliff face, some dozen yards away from them. "There's a cave. Maybe we can get the trucks inside it and out of the wind entirely."

Connolly slapped Grimes on the shoulder. "You heard the woman. Go, go!"

Grimes was already steering in that direction and moments later they slammed to a stop just outside their destination. Annja pulled the neck of her T-shirt up over her nose and mouth and then pushed her door open.

The wind was already much stronger than she expected, nearly tearing the door from her grasp. It was only with considerable effort that she managed to slam it shut again behind her. Once she had, she turned and forced her way the last few yards against the storm to the cave mouth, ducking low to enter it.

She saw immediately that it was more of a protected hollow than an actual cave. It was longer than it was deep and the ceiling overhead was so low that she had to walk in a stoop. On the plus side, however, the overhang out front hung nearly all the way down to her waist, which would help to keep the storm out. And the air inside seemed musty but breathable.

It would have to do.

Annja turned and made her way back to the Land Cruiser, fighting against the wind the entire way. As she drew closer Grimes lowered the window a crack so they could hear her, but even then she had to shout to be heard over the howl of the storm.

"Pull forward about twenty feet and park as close to the face of the ridge as you can," she told him. "The Cruisers will keep out most of the dust and wind. I'll direct the others in behind you."

Grimes nodded, rolled up the window and then did as she suggested. Annja turned and gestured for the next vehicle, repeating her instructions to the driver when he reached her. After that the other drivers got the hint; all Annja had to do was wave them forward and they followed suit, pulling in behind the others. Their passengers quickly disembarked, pulling their packs into the narrow shelter with them just in case their stay ended up being a protracted one.

Annja was about to join them when she realized they had a problem.

One of the Cruisers was missing.

She did a quick count, just to be sure, but came up short the second time, as well.

If they got stuck in this storm…

Annja took a few steps back in the direction the caravan had come from and peered through the blowing sands, looking for the missing vehicle. She finally saw it halfway down the last dune. It was skewed at an angle and, even as she watched, the Cruiser slid a few feet farther sideways until it hung there, perpendicular to the slope of the hill.

Annja headed toward them, not yet certain what she was going to do to help once she got there but knowing she had to do something. She couldn't just leave them there at the mercy of the storm.

She had to hunch forward against the force of the storm as she struggled to put one foot in front of the other and to keep herself moving in the general direction of the stuck vehicle. Twice she was knocked over and had to fight her way back to her feet. It didn't take a genius to know that getting back to the shelter was going to be twice as difficult.

She wasn't the only one having difficulty, though. She was just getting back to her feet after being knocked to the ground for the second time when the worst of her fears came to pass. A gust of wind swept down the hill and struck the Cruiser broadside. All that surface area acted like a huge sail and the force of the wind rocked the vehicle up on one set of wheels.

Annja watched in horror as it hung there for a moment and then tipped the rest of the way over, rolling over and over again as it plunged down the slope to come to a crashing halt against the hard surface of the wadi floor.

14

The sound of crashing glass and crumpled steel could barely be heard over the wind as it whipped at Annja, trying its best to turn her aside. She stared through the storm at the overturned vehicle. They could be seriously hurt in there. She began to run.

The storm was upon them in earnest now and her run quickly turned to a jog and then to a strained walk. The sand and grit stung her face and she was having difficulty breathing even through her T-shirt. Still, she fought her way forward.

The Cruiser had come to rest with the driver's side down against the earth and the wheels sticking out sideways like the legs of some dead insect. The wind was so strong, the dust so thick in the air, she walked right into one of the wheels.

Keeping one hand against the side of the truck, she traced her way along the vehicle until she reached the rear door. She was fumbling for the handle when the door opened beneath her touch and a pair of hands pulled her inside, out of the wind.

When her eyes had adjusted to the difference in light inside the vehicle, Annja found Mike and Susan crouched in the cargo space with her, relief on their faces.

"I knew you'd come!" Susan exclaimed. Then her expression turned grave. "Benjamin's hurt—I'm not sure how bad."

Annja looked over her shoulder to where Benjamin was stretched out flat on what was now the floor of the vehicle, a bloodstained bandage wrapped around his head. He gave her a weak wave and a half smile, which was a good sign. At least he was awake.

"Camera case wasn't strapped down," Mike said in a low voice. "When we rolled, it hit him. He bled a lot, but I don't think the wound is deep."

"All right," Annja said, "I've come to get you out of here before the sand buries us. But if we don't hurry, we're not going to make it to the others."

Susan immediately began to gather her things, but Mike hesitated. "Wait a minute," he said. "Why would we want to go out in that?" He pointed out the window at the now pitch-dark storm on the other side of the glass. "It's safe enough here. Why don't we just wait until the storm blows over? Surely we could dig our way out if we get buried."

Annja was already shaking her head. "You said it

yourself—you don't know how badly injured Benjamin is. One of the security team members is also a medic."

Mike grumbled, but finally agreed. Annja was going to need his size and strength to get Benjamin through the storm.

"All right," she said, "here's what we're going to do."

A few minutes later they were crowded by the back door, ready to make a break for it. Annja was first, then Susan, Benjamin and finally Mike bringing up the rear. Annja had taken a length of rope out of the supply pack and tied them together, one after another with about three feet of rope in between each person. "Lock hands once we get outside and just keep following the person in front of you," she said. "It isn't far. We just have to keep moving."

The wind nearly ripped the door out of her hands as she opened it, so she just let it go rather than injure herself trying to fight Mother Nature. With one last look back Annja headed out into the storm.

The wind was far worse now than it had been fifteen minutes before and Annja had a hard time just standing upright. She bent over as far as she dared against the worst of the gusts and pushed on.

Visibility had sunk to little better than a few inches in front of her face and for a brief moment Annja considered turning right back around and waiting out the storm in the ruined SUV. But only for a moment.

They struggled forward. The wind pushed at them and tried to steal the air out of their lungs, as if it had suddenly become some malevolent force. Annja kept her focus, putting one foot in front of the other, not letting go of Susan's hand no matter what. If she could do those two things, she would get them out of this alive.

Several times they fell, sometimes singly and sometimes as a group, and Annja was grateful for the rope that held them together.

They'd been walking for what felt like forever. Annja began to worry. *We should have reached the others by now,* she thought.

Twice more the wind knocked them off their feet and the last time Annja lay there, exhausted.

We're lost, she realized. *Must have gotten off track somewhere, wandered right past them in the storm.*

She lifted her head, but couldn't see anything through the twisting, turning sand.

As she climbed to her feet she had no idea which way to go.

They were in serious trouble.

Please. She dragged Susan to her feet behind her. *Please help us.*

Then, as if in answer to her plea, a sound intruded over the wind. It was faint, but recognizable.

A car horn.

Someone was leaning on the horn of one of the trucks.

Annja didn't say anything. The others wouldn't have heard her over the storm. She turned in the direction of the truck and began plodding forward once more, aiming for the makeshift beacon.

The horn saved their lives. Ten minutes later the bulk of the Land Cruisers materialized out of the gloom before her and then hands were reaching out to them and pulling them through the gap between the trucks and into the shelter beyond.

Annja stumbled over to a clear space and slid down the wall. She watched as Hamilton tended to Benjamin's head wound, washing with water from his canteen and then wrapping long strips of gauze around his head like a scarf. When he was finished, he tried to make the young archaeologist as comfortable as possible. It still remained to be seen whether or not they were going to need to airlift him out, but Hamilton didn't think so, which Annja took as a good sign.

Ephraim sat next to her. He had a self-satisfied look on his face and it didn't take Annja long to figure out why.

"Thank you," she told him.

He shrugged. "Grimes suggested it. I just happened to be the one sitting there behind the wheel."

"Either way, that horn saved our lives, Ephraim. So thank you."

He beamed and for the first time in an hour Annja began to feel as if everything was going to be all right.

There was little for the group to do, huddled up against the back wall as they were, trying to stay as far from the gritty, blowing air, and many of them dropped off into an uneasy sleep as they waited for it to pass, Annja among them.

15

The storm lasted just over three hours. Annja would later find out that it was one of the strongest sandstorms to strike the Negev Desert in three decades. For now all she knew was that she was damned uncomfortable being cooped up inside a shallow cave for so long. She had sand in places she hoped never to have sand again. Her only consolation was that everyone else appeared to be as uncomfortable as she was.

She rose to her feet, spat to try to clear the grit from her mouth—to no avail—and then assessed where they were. In the dim light she could see that some of the others were also shaking off the dust and trying to pull themselves together. Grimes and a few of his men were working on digging them out. The blowing sand had piled up against their vehicles, spilling around the sides and in between them. Thankfully the trucks had kept most of it out of their hidey-hole. Before joining those trying to dig them free, Annja stepped over to Benjamin.

"How are you doing?" she asked.

He grinned ruefully up at her from his spot on the floor. "I've got a whopper of a headache, but otherwise I'm okay. Might wear my seat belt next time."

She laughed, then clapped him on his good shoulder.

Even with six of them digging it took over an hour to clear the vehicles sufficiently to drive away from the cave. Two of the trucks had flat tires from flying debris. Changing them, especially on loose, uneven ground like this, was going to take some time and care.

Grimes cursed a blue streak, but there wasn't anything he could do except work on solving the problem. They created a redundant system by using two jacks on each vehicle. Should one fail, the other should keep the truck from crashing into the sand and possibly injuring anybody. It took another hour to take care of the tires, but at last they were finished.

While the security crew had been working on the trucks, Annja and the others did what they could to salvage supplies and gear from Ben's ruined vehicle, including the mostly full tank of gas. When they were done they split the load, including the extra passengers, between the other five vehicles and headed off.

The long ride passed without further incident and the sun was just setting as they arrived in the vicinity of the ruins of Ben Baraket, an ancient Hebrew trading center. In the failing light, the decision was made to camp in the lee of the ridgeline where the ruins stood and investigate the site in the morning.

The trucks were arranged facing outward with the tents in a semicircle on the inside, just as they had been the night before. Their concern about being followed had diminished but wasn't forgotten. The fact that they were cherry-picking sites to investigate and not dealing with them in the order they presented on the scroll eased their anxiety, as did the belief that no one could have tracked them through the fury of the day's storm. Still, Annja thought it wise not to dismiss the possibility outright.

The mood around the campfire that night was subdued. The day's events and Benjamin's injury had stolen some of their enthusiasm. Annja wasn't concerned, though. She knew a good night's sleep would go a long way to bringing back their excitement. And the minute they found the next cache, and at this point she was all but certain they would, they would be back to their old selves.

ONE MINUTE SHE WAS sound asleep, the next wide awake as her body's natural alarm system told her she was in danger. She lay there in her sleeping bag, eyes wide open, her body tensed and ready for action. Her heart was pounding in her chest but she kept her breathing steady and even, not wanting to give away the fact that she was no longer asleep.

Instinct told her she wasn't alone.

She lay there, straining to hear the slightest sound.

There. The sound of the zipper on the front of her tent slowly being unzipped.

That must have been what had woken her.

Camp etiquette was straightforward. You didn't enter the private quarters of another team member without first announcing yourself and waiting for a reply. Especially at this late hour.

Whoever it was, they were up to no good. That seemed clear.

A voice in the back of her mind was screaming at her to do something, but Annja bided her time, waiting for the right moment. She didn't want to spook whoever it was into running. She'd never figure this mystery out if the person managed to disappear into the darkness surrounding the camp.

Lying there, her back to the tent entrance, wasn't easy.

Steady, Annja, steady.

She heard the whisper of the tent flap being drawn aside and then the brush of fabric against the side wall of the entrance.

Steady…

Now!

She rolled over, calling her sword to her at the same time and thrusting upward toward the looming shape above her even as the sword was still forming in her hand.

To her surprise, the intruder turned his body away from her thrust, almost as if he were expecting her to make that very move. The sword slipped past him and then he was inside her range and dropping on top of her, trying to use the weight of his body to pin her to the ground while he shoved a cloth at her face.

Annja turned her head, taking the cloth on her cheek instead of over her nose and mouth. It was covered with a foul-smelling liquid and even the brief whiff she got made her dizzy. Alarms began shrieking in the back of her head as she realized the intruder was trying to drug her into unconsciousness!

She twisted her hips and thrashed her legs, trying to get out from beneath him. She was only partially successful, ending up with him kneeling between her legs, his elbows on her chest as he fought to clamp the cloth over her face. His weight bore down on her diaphragm, forcing the air out of her lungs. She ignored it for the time being, knowing the greater threat was in his hands. She grabbed his wrists, preventing him from smothering her. He tried to pull away but she held on tight. As long as she controlled his movement she'd have a much better chance of getting out of this alive.

In the dim light she couldn't see much, just had the sense of him looming over her, and so she was completely unprepared when he smacked his forehead into her own. Pain washed over her, but she held on grimly through it, determined not to let go. When he pulled himself back to try to do it again, she made her move. She shoved his right arm against his body, which caused his shoulder to dip lower and provided the opening she was looking for. In a flash she jerked her hips off the floor and wrapped her legs around his shoulders, crossing her feet at the ankles to lock them in place. He struggled to get free, but his left arm was now pinned beneath her leg, limiting his options. That didn't stop him from flailing with his right, though, and Annja felt her grip starting to loosen as the extra weight on her chest made it more and more difficult to breathe.

Now or never.

Annja released her hold on her assailant's hand and grabbed the back of his head with both of her own, shoving his chin down toward his chest. As soon as she had managed that she shifted her hip to the right, brought her right leg up higher so that it crossed over the back of his neck rather than his shoulders and locked her feet back together again, putting him into a triangle choke hold between her powerful legs.

Now all she had to do was hold tightly until he passed out.

That's when his flailing hand finally found her face and slapped that foul-smelling cloth over her mouth and nostrils.

16

Annja fought to keep from inhaling, despite her lungs already being depleted of air from her assailant's weight. He pressed the cloth down tighter and she responded by squeezing her legs together.

From that point it became a race to see who could hold out longer without air, Annja or her assailant. Her lungs were already burning and her body was starting to protest—her lizard brain telling her to take a breath while her rational brain was yelling at her not to even think about doing it.

Annja rocked her hips one way and then quickly shifted back the other, using the momentum she generated and her opponent's own weight against him to send him crashing to the ground. The motion dislodged his hand from her face and she gulped down a lungful of air as she squeezed tighter with her legs. His flailing grew weaker…and weaker…and then stopped altogether as his body went slack.

She held on for another moment, to make sure that

he wasn't faking it, and then scrambled away from the unconscious form. Her hands were shaking from all the adrenaline that had flooded her system as she called her sword and then used her free hand to snatch up the electric lantern from the corner. She flicked the switch with her thumb.

Light flooded the tent, showing her a dark-haired, bearded man unconscious across her sleeping bag. He was dressed in what looked to her to be traditional Bedouin garb—a sleeveless vest and long flowing tunic over loose-fitting trousers. If she had to guess his age she would have put him in his mid-thirties.

Who the hell was he and what did he want?

Cautiously, she stepped closer and prodded him with the edge of her blade. He didn't react. She poked him again, harder this time, but again he failed to react. Satisfied that he was actually unconscious and therefore no longer an immediate threat, she squatted next to him and rolled him over. She studied his face for a long moment.

She didn't know him

Was this one of Ephraim's infamous Gibborim?

Annja quickly searched him, looking for anything that might help her understand who he was or why he would try to kidnap her in the middle of the night, but came up empty. She did, however, notice his boots. Instead of the typical Bedouin footwear, this man was wearing what looked to her to be a pair of good old American combat boots.

What on earth?

She was moving to take a closer look when a noise from outside caught her attention. She doused the light, waited a moment for her eyes to adjust and then peered out through the open flap of her tent. She didn't see anything unusual.

Of course, that didn't mean there wasn't anything out there.

She debated keeping her sword out for a few seconds before finally deciding against it. If the noise she'd heard was nothing, she'd have a hard time explaining the three-foot broadsword. If, on the other hand, it turned out her assailant hadn't come alone, she could always call the weapon back to her with the speed of thought.

She let the sword vanish back into the otherwhere and then stepped out of the tent. Around her, the rest of the camp seemed quiet, peaceful. The other tents were dark, including the one Connolly shared with Grimes. The fire had burned down so far that even the coals were barely glowing.

It's too quiet.

No sooner had the thought formed than a dark shape came thundering out of the night toward her. It took a moment for her eyes to make sense of what she was seeing, and by the time she had, the horse and rider had crossed nearly half the distance that separated them. The rider was dressed like the first man had been, the edges of his desert robes whipping behind him as his horse charged forward. The ends of his kuffiya had been pulled around his face, hiding all of his features except his eyes. Both his horse and his clothing were black, allowing him to blend in with the shadows and no doubt accounting for the way he seemed to appear out of thin air.

But what really caught Annja's attention was the wicked-looking curved blade the rider held in his right hand.

The horse's hooves pounded the earth as it charged toward her. The rider rose slightly in his saddle, preparing to deliver a blow with his sword.

A glance beyond him revealed additional riders just now emerging into the light, spread out in an arc designed to envelop the camp. The thought that there had been a sentry posted out beyond the camp in that direction flashed into her mind.

Time seemed to slow down as she went into fight mode. Every beat of the horse's hooves against the stony ground seemed to echo in her head, timed to match the pounding of her heart.

It was immediately obvious that her options were extremely limited. If she turned her back she'd be run down in seconds. There was no way she could get out of the way before the riders reached her. Dodging to the left or right would only put her in a position to be attacked by the next rider in line.

She really only had one choice.

Stand and fight.

At the very least she could probably delay the lead

rider long enough for others to wake up and try to defend themselves.

So be it.

She stepped away from the tent, moving onto open ground, giving herself as much room to maneuver as possible. "Help! We're under attack!"

Without waiting to see if anyone heard her, she stepped forward to face the oncoming threat. She didn't know it, but she was smiling as she set her feet and prepared to meet the rider bearing down on her.

Annja could see the horse's eyes glistening in the moonlight. Her first instinct was to bring the rider down by taking out his horse, but at the last second she couldn't. She couldn't punish the animal for doing what it had been bred to do. So she changed her position and prepared to deal with the rider himself.

He raced toward her, trying to spook her into running, but she held her ground. He guided his horse slightly to his left so that he would pass her on his right. His arm drew back.

The rider was ten feet away now.

Five.

Three.

Annja had a moment to take a deep breath and then horse and rider were upon her, the sword whistling down toward her unprotected head even as she sprang her trap and called her own weapon. The broadsword appeared in her hands as if by magic. One moment the rider was bearing down on an unarmed woman and the next that same woman was stepping inside his attack and bringing a hardened steel blade up to meet his descending one in a savage blow of her own.

The rider was completely unprepared for her to turn the tables on him, and the unexpected strike, combined with the force of the blow, sent him toppling off the horse's back in a heap.

Annja didn't give him a chance to recover. As he pushed up from the ground, she ran him through with her sword. He gave a surprised grunt and died, a bewildered expression on his face. Annja felt no remorse. He'd tried to kill her—and no doubt would have succeeded if she'd remained weaponless.

She pulled her sword free.

Chaos swirled on all sides of her.

While she dealt with the first rider, the others had passed her and reached the center of the camp. Her warning had succeeded in rousing some of the security team, however, who were now locked in combat with the horsemen. Annja tried to make sense of it all. Images flashed through her mind as if she were seeing them with the help of a strobe light.

Flash.

A rider rearing up over one of Grimes's men who was trying to scramble out of his tent. The rider's sword flashing downward as the other man frantically sought to draw his gun.

Flash.

Two security agents pulling a rider down from his saddle and falling on him, their fists flying.

Flash.

Grimes stepping inside the arc of his opponent's sword, catching him by the arm and twisting suddenly, sending the other man over his head in a classic judo throw before leaping on him, a knife glinting in his hand.

Flash.

Two swordsmen advancing on Connolly, who stood in front of his tent holding them off with nothing more than a shovel in his hands....

That last image was enough to snap her back into action. Annja raced toward the group even as the swordsmen took their first swings at Connolly. Miraculously he managed to evade both blows, deflecting the strikes with the blade of the shovel as he frantically backpedaled.

No one noticed Annja advancing from behind, least of all the swordsmen, and she drew close enough to strike before anyone even knew she was there. Her first blow struck the rearmost swordsman's head from his shoulders in a spray of arterial blood.

His death provided a warning to his partner, who turned to meet Annja with a flurry of sword thrusts. In seconds she was fighting for her life against an opponent who clearly knew how to use the weapon in his hands. He came at her aggressively, trying to use his strength and size to overwhelm her in the first few mo-

ments of their encounter. But Annja was far too good
with a sword to fall for something as simple as that. She
parried each swing and then went on an offensive of her
own, slashing and jabbing and thrusting at her opponent, driving him backward…right to where Connolly
was waiting with the shovel. Annja thought she could
hear the crack of bone as the shovel hit its target and
the swordsman collapsed with a crushed skull.

Annja was about to go help the others when Connolly shouted, "The map!" Turning, he raced inside his
tent. Afraid to leave him alone, she moved to follow
him inside, but not before letting her own sword vanish back into the otherwhere and replacing it with one
of the attacker's weapons lying nearby. She could only
hope that Connolly wouldn't notice that her sword was
now curved where moments before it had been straight.

Inside the tent Annja found him unlocking one of
the large chests to the left of the folding safari cot he
was using as a bed.

"Thank God you came along when you did, Annja."
He opened the trunk and began moving things around
inside. "I found those bastards trying to sneak inside the
tent just after you sounded the alarm and held them off
as long as I could. But things were getting a bit dicey
there, I don't mind saying. Another few minutes…"

Another few minutes and you would have been toast.
No one needed to be reminded of their own mortality,
least of all the billionaire who was funding their expedition.

She cast an anxious glance back toward the entrance to the tent, knowing that there were probably others who needed their help.

"Ah!" Connolly brandished the leather case containing his iPad over his head as he stood. "They didn't get it."

That was all Annja needed to see. "Stay here and don't leave the tent until Grimes or I tell you its safe!" She dashed back out.

She emerged from the tent to find the mysterious riders retreating as quickly as they had come, disappearing into the darkness on the far side of the camp.

17

Just like that, it was over. Annja and the others were left staring into the darkness where the horsemen had disappeared, wondering what had just happened.

Grimes took control of the situation, ordering those who were healthy to tend to the wounded after he did a quick head count. Amazingly, they'd only lost two—Chan, who had been on guard duty at the time of the attack and had no doubt died before he knew what hit him, and Mendez, the man Annja had seen murdered as he'd struggled to get out of his tent. A few of the others had minor scrapes and injuries, but nothing a first aid kit couldn't treat.

They had killed three of the attackers in turn—the horseman Annja had taken out early in the battle, the one crushed by Connolly's shovel and the man Grimes had killed with his knife. They also had one captive, now tied and gagged—the man Annja had choked into unconsciousness during the first moments of the attack. A quick search of both their captive and the bodies of his comrades didn't turn up anything that could help identify who they were.

Grimes wasn't ready to let it go at that, however.

"We need to go after them and we need to do it now," he was saying to Connolly as Annja walked over after checking on Ephraim and the others. "It's going to be a while before our new 'guest' is able to tell us anything and we can't afford to give them time to regroup and attack again. The best thing we can do is move in on them, just as they did to us."

"You think they'll be back?" Connolly asked.

"Of course I do. They want something from us and won't stop until they get it. We need to know more about them so that we don't give them the opportunity to try a stunt like this again."

Grimes was right—they needed to know as much about their opponents as possible because she was as certain as he was that this wasn't the last they'd see of them. The riders would be back. She had no doubt about that. A little knowledge would go a long way in helping them prepare to deal with them when the time came.

Connolly, as it turned out, didn't need much convincing.

Once the decision was made to go after them, the group wasted no time in getting under way. Grimes ordered Johnson and Daniels to stay behind and guard the camp in case the intruders came back. Ephraim herded the graduate students into one tent, where he could watch over all of them during the remainder of the night. For once, none of them complained. Meanwhile, Grimes, Connolly, Annja and the other four security guards would pursue the horsemen out into the desert in the hopes of locating their camp and learning why the group attacked them in the first place.

"The Gibborim take their mission very seriously, Annja," Ephraim told her quietly, out of earshot of the others. "Perhaps it is best if you remain behind, here, with us. Where it is safe."

"It's not the Gibborim I'm worried about," she replied. "It's Connolly and his men."

She wasn't kidding, either. The attack on the camp had brought out a militaristic attitude in Connolly and his team that was making her nervous. She had a nagging feeling they knew more than they were letting on about what was happening. Annja didn't like being in the dark and had no intention of letting them keep her at arm's length.

"Don't worry, Ephraim," she told him. "I can take care of myself."

She wondered what he would think of her if he really knew what she was capable of.

One of the security guards in the hunters' group, a young black fellow by the name of Gardner, had spent two tours in the mountains of Afghanistan hunting the Taliban and so Grimes ordered him to take point. His teammates—Beck, Hamilton and Douglas—would be on foot behind him so that they formed a wide diamond. Behind them would come Grimes, Connolly and Annja in one of the SUVs, without headlights. Gardner would be using a red-colored flashlight to follow the horses' tracks and they didn't want to mess up his night vision or give their location away to the enemy.

They would have to travel slowly, as a result, but the consensus seemed to be that the camp wouldn't be far. The raiders probably wouldn't expect their targets to come after them and, if they were the Gibborim as Ephraim feared, then they would remain close enough to keep the treasure hunters under observation.

They took their previous positions—Grimes behind the wheel, Annja in the front passenger seat, Connolly in back behind Grimes. The atmosphere was tense as they peered out into the night, trying to keep the security team in sight while at the same time trying to avoid driving into a boulder or sliding into a ditch.

Just over an hour passed before Gardner held up a clenched fist and they all stopped. Beck, Hamilton and Douglas took up defensive positions around the front of the vehicle, facing forward, while Gardner came back to talk to Grimes.

"There's a ridge up ahead," he whispered through the open window. "I can make out the light of a camp-fire coming from the other side."

"Well, then let's go take a look," Grimes said.

They got out of the car, easing the doors shut behind them. Grimes produced a pair of automatic pistols from somewhere, checked to be sure they were loaded and then passed one to Connolly without a word. Since

the security detail were carrying M4 carbines, that left
Annja the only one in the group without a firearm. Fine
with her. She had her own weapon should she need it.

The security team fanned out around the three of
them, resuming their diamond formation, but this time
with Connolly, Grimes and Annja in the center. Moving
slowly and quietly, the group made its way up the ridgeline. Camp sounds could be heard as they drew closer
to the top—men's voices, the clank of pots knocking
against one another, the nicker of horses. When Gardner gave the signal, they got down on their bellies and
crawled the rest of the way to the top. From that vantage
point, they looked down into the wadi on the other side.

Gardner had lived up to his reputation and taken
them right to the raiders' camp. Annja counted twelve
men around the fire below them, their horses tied up
nearby. They appeared to be armed—some with the
curved swords they'd used during the attack on the archaeologists' camp less than an hour before and some
with what appeared to be Kalashnikov semiautomatic
rifles. The ever-popular AK-47s, if she had to guess. A
few of them were tending to the wounds of those who
had been injured in the fight, but most of them seemed
to be arguing with a man who appeared to be their
leader. He was clearly in disagreement with whatever
it was the others were saying. They were too far away
to hear clearly, but Annja thought they were speaking
in…French? Finally fed up, the leader turned and dis-

appeared inside a brightly colored tent that stood at a distance from the others.

Annja leaned toward Grimes. "Now what?" she whispered. She didn't think they were going to learn much from up here. It was starting to look like this had been a bad idea.

Grimes ignored her question. Instead, he whispered, "Stay here and guard Connolly," and then signaled for his men to follow him. Annja didn't even have a moment to object as they slipped into the darkness. She moved to go after them but was brought up short when Connolly grabbed her arm in an unexpectedly powerful grip. He shook his head.

This was supposed to be a reconnaissance, not a damned search-and-destroy mission. Just what on earth did Grimes think he was doing?

From her position on the ridge, Annja was able to watch as Grimes's men encircled the camp and then moved in silently from all directions, their weapons at the ready. For a moment she thought they would take the camp without bloodshed, that the security team would get close enough to make resistance an obviously futile idea, but then a shout went up from one of the Bedouins who, rather than surrendering, went for his gun.

Big mistake.

Grimes's men opened fire with short, controlled bursts from their M4s and the desert raiders went down in a haze of bullets. It was done with such brutal efficiency that Annja realized she had vastly underestimated the security team's capabilities. She'd assumed they were your typical executive protection detail, but from the way they'd just taken out the entire camp in a matter of seconds she guessed they were much more than that. Not just ex-military, but most likely ex–Special Forces.

She didn't find the revelation particularly comforting.

The gunfire drew the Bedouin leader back out of his tent. He rushed into the center of the camp, drawing his pistol as he came, only to find himself surrounded. For a moment Annja thought he was going to try to fight. One man armed with a pistol against Grimes's security team armed with semiautomatic rifles. But his good sense must have asserted itself and before the others opened fire the man raised his hands over his head.

Grimes looked at Hamilton and inclined his head toward the surrendering man. While Grimes covered him with his pistol, Hamilton moved in, disarmed the other man and then forced him down on his knees with his hands over his head. Grimes gave the signal for the others to stand down. While Hamilton kept a gun trained on the prisoner, the others relaxed and lowered their weapons.

Then, and only then, did Grimes signal for Annja and Connolly to join them.

It took a few minutes to clamber down from the ridge and, by the time Annja arrived in the camp, the bodies of the raiders had been dragged to one side and lined up in a row.

Eleven men dead in moments.

Annja didn't like it at all. But something told her that now would not be a good time to object to what had just happened.

It wouldn't take much for you to end up lying right there with the Bedouins.

The ruthless manner in which the desert raiders had been dispatched brought her earlier concerns back tenfold. She'd underestimated the security team's role in this enterprise and it made her wonder what else she had missed. This entire expedition was rapidly moving in a direction she wasn't comfortable with.

"Give me a few minutes," Grimes said to Connolly, "and we'll know everything we need to about their interest in us, sir."

Connolly surprised them with his reply. "No. I want to talk to him myself."

Grimes frowned. "That's not a good idea."

"I don't care," Connolly replied. He strode forward, forcing Grimes to follow him or be left out of earshot. Annja tagged along, as well.

Connolly stood looking down at the prisoner kneeling on the ground before him. The other man gazed up at him, his expression unreadable.

"Who are you? What are you doing here?" Connolly asked in English.

The prisoner didn't respond.

Connolly tried again, this time in Hebrew. Annja didn't speak the language, but she recognized it and assumed he'd asked the same two questions.

Again no response.

By the time Connolly asked a third time, in what sounded to Annja like Arabic, the prisoner had apparently grown bored and glanced at the rest of them. His expression didn't change as his gaze passed over Grimes, but when he looked at Annja he hesitated for the barest fraction of a moment before glancing away.

Annja knew that it could have been the fact that she was the only woman among a group of men that caught the prisoner's attention, but her instincts were telling her it was something more than that.

She stepped forward and put her hand on Connolly's arm, just as he was opening his mouth to say something else. He stiffened at her touch but didn't pull away as he glanced at her.

"May I try?" she asked.

Connolly grunted.

The prisoner smirked as she stepped in front of him. She fixed her gaze on his.

"We know who you are so there's no sense in lying about it," she said in French.

There.

For just a fraction of a second the man's pupils had widened before he'd glanced away, seemingly indifferent to what she'd said.

But Annja knew better. He'd understood her.

She was about to say something to that effect to Connolly when she abruptly changed her mind. There was something here that she was missing, something important.

She pretended to try again, asking the man his name in both Italian and Spanish before giving up with a shrug of her shoulders.

The others apparently had had enough, as well. Connolly exchanged a few words with Grimes privately before the latter turned back to Hamilton and, pointing to a spot on the edge of camp away from everything else, said, "Take him over there and sit on him until we're ready to go."

"Got it, boss." Hamilton grabbed the other man's arm and hauled him to his feet. "Let's go, knucklehead."

That's when everything fell apart.

The prisoner's docility throughout the interrogation had lulled Hamilton into thinking he was no longer a threat, so when he sprang into action, kicking Hamilton's knee joint with a side kick, the guard was unable to protect himself. Hamilton went down screaming, his knee badly twisted by the blow. The prisoner spun around, but rather than trying to make a run for it he dropped to one knee and thrust his hand inside the lip of his boot. When it came out again, he was holding a squat-looking pistol that Annja didn't recognize but that she knew was as lethal as it was ugly.

Time slowed.

The Bedouin's hand began to come up, the barrel of the pistol pointed in Connolly's direction.

Annja was already in motion, having thrown herself at Connolly the moment she'd seen what was in the other man's hand.

Dimly, she heard Grimes yelling something, but it seemed to be coming from very far away and she couldn't make out what it was.

A shot rang out.

Everything sped back up again as Annja slammed into Connolly, the two of them tumbling to the ground even as the bullet sped through the spot where Connolly had been standing a split second before. Annja hit the ground hard, the impact driving the air out of her lungs. She forced herself to roll to one side, waiting for the gunman's next shot, the one that wouldn't miss.

But when the gunshots came they were from Grimes and his companions rather than the Bedouin leader, the chatter of their semiautomatic weapons filling the air with thunder. Bullets chewed into the man, making his body spasm and dance beneath their force, and he went over backward to lie still in the dirt without pulling the trigger a second time.

For a long moment no one moved, as if afraid to break the stillness, and then Grimes was kicking the ground in his frustration.

They'd wanted the Bedouin leader alive. It was the only way they were going to get answers. Of course, the Bedouin had known that, as well, and rather than submit, he'd made sure he wouldn't be in any condition to talk.

She had to hand it to him—it was an elegant way out of a messy situation.

Grimes stalked over to the man's corpse and nudged him with his boot. When he didn't move, Grimes bent down, rolled the man over on his back and verified that he was, indeed, dead. Grimes quickly searched him, but came up empty. He rose but stood over the body for a moment, staring down at the man's tanned face.

Annja watched curiously, wondering what Grimes was looking for, and so was able to react quicker than anyone else when Grimes drew his knife and bent over the body a second time.

"Wait a minute, Grimes," Annja said, concerned he was going to do something unpleasant to the corpse, but her fears turned out to be misplaced. Grimes didn't take the knife to the corpse, just to the corpse's clothing.

He pulled the man's tunic away from his chest and then sawed down through it. The threads made small little popping noises as they gave way beneath the blade. Grimes spread the fabric apart, exposing the flesh beneath.

Where the skin of the man's face and hands was deeply tanned, his chest was a pale, fish-belly white, as if he hadn't spent much time in the sun at all.

"Someone get me a rag," Grimes said over his shoulder and a few moments later one was pushed into his hand. He worked up a mouthful of saliva, spat on the rag and then squatted beside the body. Holding the man's head steady with one hand, he used the other to scrub at the man's forehead. After a moment or two of effort, he stopped.

"I knew it!" Grimes said in disgust as he climbed to his feet and stepped away to let the others survey his handiwork.

Annja glanced at the body. Where Grimes had wiped at the man's flesh with the rag, a circle of pale skin was now plain to see.

18

"What the hell?" Connolly muttered, staring down at the corpse along with the rest of them. "What's going on, Grimes?"

"We're being played, that's what's going on." Grimes kicked at the dirt.

Annja knew how he felt. She didn't like being played any more than the next guy, particularly over something like this. Clearly someone had been using the ancient legend of the Giborrim, the guardians of the treasure, in an attempt to scare them off. She, of all people, should have seen through that right from the start. She wasn't *Chasing History's Monsters'* resident skeptic for nothing. But the story—supported by Ephraim, who she respected—had started to get under her skin.

Someone outside their group was aware what they were doing here and was determined to keep them from finding more of the treasure. Most likely so that they—whoever "they" were—could claim it for their own. If they could get their hands on the scroll's clues.

And if the treasure wasn't enough of an incentive, Annja had no doubt Connolly himself had hundreds of rivals who would like nothing more than to see the man fail.

"All right," Grimes told his men, once they'd gotten a look at the so-called Bedouin. "I want to know who these guys are and what they were up to. Get to it!"

The bodies were searched to no avail. The tents, however, were another story.

If there were any doubts remaining that the group had been masquerading as Bedouins, they were effectively dispelled the minute the team found modern clothing and camping gear—everything from mummy bags to freeze-dried concentrates. The labels had either been cut out or scoured free from most of the equipment and those few pieces that did still have some kind of branding, such as the packets of dehydrated food, came from companies that distributed worldwide. As such, they didn't provide them with any real information that could be used to identify the assailants.

Things got even more interesting when Grimes and Annja turned their attention to the leader's tent. Inside they found the same collection of modern amenities, with the addition of state-of-the-art radio gear. What caught their attention, though, was the collection of photographs pinned to the canvas walls of the tent.

They were all black-and-white, about twenty images in all. Judging from the graininess of the images, they had been taken from some distance away.

Each and every one of the photographs was of Annja.

They had been taken at various times of the day—some in the morning, some in the afternoon, a few of them as the sun was going down in the background—but they were consistent in that all of them had been taken during the current expedition, starting almost from the moment the team had left Jerusalem. The first few showed Annja inside the Land Cruiser as they drove out of the city, and from the angle of the image she guessed they been taken from a rooftop overlooking the street. Others showed her working at the first dig site—helping unearth the jars of coins they'd found, and later, laughing around the campfire during dinner. There were even a few of her standing watching Grimes's men change the tires flattened by the sandstorm.

That she'd been under surveillance that long sent chills down her spine.

"Well, at least we know they don't want you dead," Grimes said absently, studying one of the shots.

"Why do you say that?"

He gestured at the photos. "The man who took these pictures could just as easily been carrying a rifle instead of a camera. At these ranges, even a semicompetent gunman would have been hard-pressed to miss."

Annja looked at the photos again and realized that Grimes was right. They could have taken her out if that had been their objective. A few years ago she might have passed off the idea as complete nonsense, but that was before she'd taken up Joan's sword. She'd made more than her share of enemies since and any one of them might want her dead. She'd never seen the cameraman, never even known he was out there, and it stood to reason that she never would have seen a gunman, either. One shot and it would have all been over.

But that shot hadn't come, which meant they didn't want her dead.

Beck stuck his head inside the tent. "Sir," he said, "you're gonna want to see this."

Annja followed Grimes outside to where Hamilton stood examining an oversize GPS unit, or at least that's what it looked like to Annja. Hamilton explained that it was a tracking device. A topographical map of the local area was currently displayed on the screen and he pointed to a blinking green dot in the center of it.

"That's us," he told them.

He did something to the controls and the image on the screen changed as the map scrolled sideways for a moment to reveal a blinking red dot.

"And that," he said, pointing at the red dot, "is a target."

Pop-ups on the lower edge of the screen gave coordinate and distance-to-the-target readings. Clearly the device was picking up a signal from the target, checking the location against a satellite-based GPS system and translating what it learned into a set of directions. It was like a navigation device for a car. All you had to do was follow the prompts on the screen to take you from one location to the other.

"Ever seen one of these before?" Grimes asked.

Beck nodded. "Pretty standard tracker. You tag the target with a beacon, switch it on so it starts broadcasting, and then use this baby—" he hefted the handheld device "—to follow it wherever it goes."

"Range?"

The younger man shrugged. "Depends on terrain, signal interference, but generally about ten miles or so."

That answered the question of how the raiders had managed to follow them from one site to the other without being seen. At some point since taking possession of the vehicles, one or more of them must have been tagged with a radio transmitter that was broadcasting their position. In this case, to fake Bedouins.

What it didn't tell them was why.

Of course, when you were unearthing a treasure worth hundreds of millions of dollars, it didn't take a Ph.D. to figure that one out.

It also didn't explain why the "Bedouins" had tried to kidnap her. And that's what it had been, she realized, a kidnapping attempt. They'd tried to take her alive before attacking the rest of the camp and she shuddered to think what might have happened to her if they had succeeded. With the rest of the expedition team slaughtered in their sleep, no one would have known she was missing until it was too late to do anything about it.

This expedition was getting more dangerous by the minute.

"Anything else?" Grimes asked.

Beck shook his head. "The latrine's freshly dug so they haven't been here very long, certainly no more than a day at most. The rest of the equipment is off-the-shelf stuff, nothing that can help us track down where it came from or who bought it."

Grimes nodded and, by his expression, Annja knew Beck's assessment was no more than he'd expected. "All right," he said, "I don't want a word of this to anyone, least of all the civilians at camp. Keep your mouths shut unless I tell you otherwise. Now sterilize the site and let's get out of here."

Sterilize the site?

It didn't take her long to discover what he meant.

The bodies of the dead were stacked inside the leader's tent, doused with gasoline from the extra tanks on the back of the Land Cruiser and set alight. More gasoline was splashed on the other tents and these, too, were set alight. The flames quickly engulfed everything. The stench was awful, but this far from civilization no one was going to come looking to investigate. By the time someone found the remains, there wouldn't be anything left to tie Grimes and his men to these men's deaths.

Except you.

Annja realized Grimes was thinking the same thing when he turned to her and said in a low voice, "This is covering your ass as well as ours, so I don't want to hear any whining about it when we get back to camp. If you've got a problem, you keep it to yourself."

"Understood."

And it was. The truth was that Annja thought the raiders had gotten what they deserved and she wasn't too broken up about it at all. She would have preferred taking them alive, if only to be able to question them about the their objectives toward her, but they had made their choice by attacking the expedition in the first place. Annja had no illusions that they would have tried again if the opportunity had presented itself. With the raiders out of the way, the expedition was that much safer.

If she was worried about anyone, it was Grimes. He'd been growing more and more militant the farther they'd gotten from civilization and this latest ruthlessness, while ultimately necessary, concerned her. She had to be ready to react. To anything.

BACK IN CAMP it took them less than ten minutes to find the tracking beacon attached to the wheel well of the middle vehicle. It was held on with a set of powerful magnets but a good, sharp tug was all it took to break it free. Grimes pulled out the battery and the signal stopped transmitting.

Simple, really.

Half an hour later, Annja sat with Ephraim in the dim light of his tent, talking quietly. She filled him in on everything that had happened since she'd left camp several hours before.

When she was finished, Ephraim sat silently for several long minutes. He seemed to be trying to take it all in. Annja didn't blame him; all that violence was difficult to get your head around if you weren't used to it.

And what does that say about her? All that violence barely even made her pause.

"Better them than us, I suppose."

Annja was surprised. It was not the response she'd been expecting.

Ephraim must have caught her expression. His self-conscious laughter had more than a hint of bitterness to it. "I've lived a long time, my dear. We Jews are no stranger to violence, especially in defense of the greater good. I trust you did everything you could. Sometimes violence happens too quickly for others to stop it, especially when one isn't ready for it."

Annja didn't respond and Ephraim was kind enough to pretend he didn't notice.

"I must say it's rather disappointing."

"What is?" she asked.

Ephraim waved his hand. "That it turned out to be men in disguise."

"As opposed to a two-millennia-old secret society?"

"Exactly! Being hunted by the Giborrim had a sense of, well, romance to it. To find they were simply men in disguise? How...ordinary."

Annja giggled. She couldn't help it. To hear the scholarly and erudite professor pine over a missed opportunity to interact with the fantastic was just too much.

Thankfully he had the grace to find himself just as amusing as she did and he joined in, the laughter a much-needed release for both of them.

They quieted after a moment, lost in their own thoughts, and then Ephraim asked, "What will they do with the prisoner?"

Annja shook her head. "I don't know for sure but my guess is that Connolly will call in his chopper again and they'll turn him over to the authorities when the opportunity arises."

"Good. A kidnapping charge is just the thing for a guy like that. If they'd caught them the first time around perhaps they wouldn't have tried again."

Annja started. Until that moment she'd been thinking about the two attempts to kidnap her as separate incidents, but now she wondered if perhaps Ephraim was right. Was the man from the museum a member of the group that had been tracking them this whole time? Is that why there were so many surveillance photos of her in the enemy leader's tent?

She went back through the attack at the Shrine of the Book. She turned the images of her attacker over in her mind, comparing them to the men she'd seen around the fire at the raider's camp earlier that evening. Were any of them a match?

She didn't think so.

Still, something nagged at her.

It was there, on the edge of her thoughts, but every time she tried to pull it into the forefront of her mind it slipped away, like a dream in the moments after awakening.

Something to do with the fight…

Whatever it was it remained just out of her grasp.

Ephraim yawned mightily, bringing her thoughts back to the here and now. It had been a long day followed by an even longer night.

"Time to get some sleep," she said, "before there isn't any more the night left."

She said good-night and returned to her tent. Most people would have been uncomfortable with sleeping in the same spot where just a few hours before someone had tried to kidnap them, but Annja had never been most people. She undressed, slipped into her sleeping bag and settled down to grab a few hours of shut-eye.

But thoughts kept returning to her encounter in the Shrine, a single question holding back the boundaries of sleep.

What am I missing?

19

"Annja! Come quick! They're going to kill him!"

The shout brought Annja out of a deep sleep and she was just in time to see Mike yank his head back out of the door of her tent and dash off. His words took a moment to filter their way through her sleep-fogged mind, but when they did she flew into action.

She threw on her clothes, slammed her feet into her hiking boots and emerged from her tent to the sounds of loud voices coming from the nearby ridge where they had located the ruins of the ancient trading center the day before. She turned and hurried in that direction.

Ephraim caught up with her as she scrambled up the path to the excavation site.

"What's going on?" he asked as he huffed to keep up with her long-legged stride.

"I don't know," she said, her gut tightening. "Stay behind me when we get up there, Ephraim, there's no telling what we'll find."

The older man didn't say anything, but she could

feel his displeasure. What was supposed to have been a professional expedition was quickly turning into a circus sideshow.

They crested the ridge and looked out over the plateau where the trading center had once been. Several of the walls still stood, and though they were little more than knee-high piles of rocks, Annja could imagine how the small community had been laid out because of them.

A larger building, perhaps a public building or synagogue, once sat near the center of the site and it was within its crumbling walls that the commotion came from.

As Annja drew closer, she saw two of Grimes's security men holding the prisoner they had captured the night before upright between them, the man's arms secured behind his back. Grimes stood in front of him with his right hand clenched tightly in a fist. The blood streaming from the prisoner's nose and the eye that was already beginning to swell told Annja that Grimes hadn't been shy about using it. Connolly stood a few paces away, watching as his second-in-command continued his work.

"I can keep asking all day, if that's what you want. I don't think you'll be in much shape to hear it after a while though, so you might as well make this easy on yourself. Where is the treasure?"

The treasure?

It was only then that Annja noticed the freshly dug trench running along the crumbling stone wall behind the four men. A large pile of earth sat at one end and marks in the dirt along the edges of the trench revealed where something heavy had been hauled up from below.

Annja couldn't believe it. Someone had unearthed the treasure in the middle of the night.

The sound of fist striking flesh drew her attention away from the hasty excavation. She turned just in time to see the prisoner spit out a mouthful of blood and broken teeth, then glare at Grimes in defiance.

"I told you," the man said in thickly accented English, "we had nothing to do with it."

Grimes hit him again.

Annja had seen enough. "Stop!" she shouted. "No more!"

Grimes barely glanced in her direction as he snarled, "This doesn't concern you, Annja, so stay out of it."

Not a chance. With her concerns from the night before still in the forefront of her mind, there was no way she was going to sit idly by while Grimes beat the tar out of a defenseless prisoner.

Grimes drew his fist back, preparing to strike again. Annja rushed forward and put herself between Grimes and the prisoner. "I said that's enough!"

Grimes was practically spitting in her face as he said, "Get out of the way, Ms. Creed, or I'm not going to be responsible for my actions. This man has information we need and I intend to get it. If I have to go through you to get it."

Her hand twitched as she fought the urge to call her sword.

Without taking her gaze off Grimes's face, she spoke over his shoulder at Connolly. "Whatever he tells you under duress isn't going to be worth garbage and you know it. There has to be a better way."

Grimes took a step closer, getting right up in her face. "This man and his buddies are responsible for killing two of my men and for hijacking our find out from under our noses. I'll be damned if I just let that go unanswered. Now get the hell out of my way or so help me—"

"Grimes."

Connolly didn't raise his voice, but his tone brought Grimes up short.

"Sir?"

"Perhaps there is a better way."

Annja turned to thank him, but he wasn't finished.

"Tie him up over there and leave him in the heat until he decides to tell us something."

"But…"

Connolly whirled to face her. "Would you prefer that I let Grimes continue?"

Annja shook her head, disconcerted by the savage look in Connolly's eyes. This was a different man from the one she'd had dinner with back in Jerusalem.

Still, she hesitated, searching her mind for an argument that might sway him, until a hand fell on her arm. She glanced over and found that Ephraim had caught up with her. There was fear in his eyes, a sense that they were perilously close to a precipice and one false step could send them plunging. He inclined his head, just the slightest nod back in the direction of the camp.

She let Ephraim lead her away, looking back over her shoulder as the prisoner was dragged to the remains of a column and tied there in a seated position, his back to the stone.

It wasn't going to take very long for the temperature to rise, and when it did, it was going to turn that cool stone into a blistering furnace. As she walked off she found herself wondering if she'd done the prisoner any favor at all.

From the look in his eyes, he was probably wondering the same thing.

20

The other members of her team were waiting outside her tent when she and Ephraim got back to camp. Susan had apparently been elected spokesperson and she wasted no time in getting to the point.

"I'm sorry, Professor, but we've had enough. It's too dangerous to stay any longer."

"You want to leave the expedition?" Ephraim asked, glancing from one to the other.

Several of them nodded. Susan said, "Yes. We want to return to Jerusalem. Today, if possible." Her voice had taken on a hard edge, as if expecting Ephraim to protest their decision.

They're scared, Annja thought, and I don't blame them. They'd signed on for an archeological dig, not to be hunted in the middle of the night by swordsmen disguised as some sect out of Jewish legend. She should have sent them home the minute she'd known there was going to be opposition to what they were doing.

Ephraim smiled. "I think that's an excellent idea."

Annja, however, was not smiling. It had just occurred to her that Connolly might not let them leave.

Only one way to find out.

"I'll talk to Connolly," Annja said, "see if he can spare one of the Land Cruisers to take you all back to Jerusalem."

To keep them occupied, Ephraim put them to work excavating a corner of one of the smaller buildings on the south side of the dig site. Annja worked along with them, enjoying the opportunity to get her hands dirty, as Ephraim liked to say. Despite their real fear, the students were eager to work a fresh site and Annja was reminded of the thrill of discovery that had gotten her into archaeology in the first place.

About an hour after they started, Annja excused herself and went to find Connolly. He was in his tent, as she had expected, and, as usual, Grimes was with him.

"With your permission, I'd like to send the graduate students back to the city."

Grimes frowned deeply as Connolly asked, "Why?"

"We've inadvertently put them in danger by bringing them along and I'd like to remedy that. We don't really need them. Ephraim and I can handle the excavation and we can use the security team to help move any heavy objects when we investigate the next site."

Connolly gave it some thought. "Grimes?"

The other man didn't hesitate. "Absolutely not."

Annja couldn't believe what she was hearing. "I'm sorry?"

Grimes watched her steadily. "I said no."

"And why is that?"

"Because we do need them. Otherwise, you wouldn't have brought them along in the first place."

Annja shook her head. "We don't need them, not enough to put their lives in danger. Or are you forgetting that we were attacked last night?" Her annoyance was rising. This shouldn't even require a discussion.

"And we dealt with the attackers appropriately, or are you forgetting that?"

Annja glared at him. "I haven't forgotten. But that doesn't mean there aren't more of them out there waiting for their own opportunity."

"Exactly my point," Grimes replied. "What if they are out there, watching us even now? Sending your colleagues back to Jerusalem alone could well result in their being ambushed along the way."

"So have one or two of the security personnel escort them back."

"And leave us more vulnerable than we are now? Not a chance. They'll just have to stick it out here with the rest of us until we're finished."

"I think they should be able to decide whether to take the risk or not."

"No," Grimes said. "I won't have them injured traveling back to Jerusalem on their own. I won't have that on my conscience, Annja."

What conscience?

Connolly lifted his hands palms out in a helpless

gesture. "I have to listen to Martin's recommendations, Annja. I'm sure you understand. For now, we stay together."

Further argument wouldn't get her anywhere, so Annja returned to the excavation area. She pulled Ephraim aside and let him know they were all going to be here awhile. Together, they broke the news to the rest of the group. As expected, they weren't happy.

Unable to ease the camp tension, Annja decided to see the prisoner...although she felt useless. There was clearly nothing she could do for him, either.

Like Grimes, she wanted some answers, but his approach was doomed to failure. A little honey would go a lot further. To that end she brought with her one of their freeze-dried meals, already reconstituted with hot water, and a bottle of Gatorade. The prisoner had been in the sun for hours now and was no doubt in need of both.

Beck was on guard duty when she arrived. Of all of Grimes's security team, Annja liked him the least. He was a hard-faced, arrogant pain in the butt who considered anyone not part of the security team to be beneath him. Annja wasn't the type to suffer such fools gladly.

He watched her approach with a smirk. "Where do you think you're going?" he asked as his eyes traveled up and down her body.

She gave him the same head-to-toe assessment but let her disdain for him plainly show. He flushed, and stood a little straighter.

"I'm going to talk to the man *I* captured," she said.

Beck shook his head. "No one's allowed to talk to the prisoner. Boss's orders."

By "boss" he meant Grimes, not Connolly, and for a moment she toyed with the idea of telling him that Connolly had sent her to interrogate the prisoner personally, but Beck was a stickler for protocol. He'd most likely call Connolly to verify his orders.

She glanced beyond Beck at the prisoner. He sat with his back to the pillar, his legs splayed out before him. He seemed to be unconscious, his head hanging limply against his chest. There was little doubt their voices would carry the short distance to where he was tied up, but he hadn't even lifted his head to see what was going on.

In fact, he hadn't moved at all since she'd arrived.

Not good.

"When was the last time he had water?" Annja asked, a creeping suspicion forming in the back of her mind.

Beck just stared at her.

Annja shoved past him to the prisoner.

He didn't move, didn't give any indication that he was even aware of her presence.

She put the food and water down next to him, then used both hands to gently lift his face up off his chest so she could take a look.

What she saw was alarming.

He'd only been in the sun for several hours but that

was apparently enough. His face was turning red and his lips were chapped and peeling. His eyes rolled in their sockets, unable to focus on her. He was barely conscious. If she hadn't been holding his head upright he wouldn't have been able to on his own.

Knowing how hot it could get at a dig site, Annja always carried a small tube of sunblock in her pocket. She pulled it out, squeezed some out and spread it on the prisoner's face and neck.

Beck hurried over, clearly upset. "What are you doing?"

"When was the last time he had anything to drink?" she asked again.

This time Beck answered her. She didn't think it had anything to do with her anger, but rather the thought of what Grimes would do to him if something happened to the prisoner on his watch. "Last night maybe?" he said.

Cursing under her breath, Annja uncapped the Gatorade and poured a little between the man's lips. At first it just dribbled back out, but then he seemed to come back to himself and managed to swallow it. Annja gave him a little more.

"Easy," she said to him in French. "Small sips."

He nodded slightly in understanding.

French, it is, then, Annja thought with a small sense of satisfaction, but she didn't let it show. Right now she was more concerned with keeping the prisoner from getting heatstroke. Clearly he wasn't used to being in the hot desert sun like this.

Beck sauntered back over to his guard station. He was still in earshot, but that was better than having him standing there all jumpy with a gun in hand. She didn't need anyone having any accidents today.

"Better?" she asked, again in French, when he had consumed almost half of the Gatorade.

He nodded, then answered in the same language, "Yes, thank you."

She glanced over at Beck. His attention was elsewhere. She fed the prisoner a few bites of the food she'd brought.

"What's your name?"

Rather than replying he simply shook his head. Apparently he wasn't willing to go down that road yet.

"Okay," she told him, "play it your way. But I can't do anything for you unless you cooperate and trust me. I'm far more agreeable than the rest of this bunch."

He still didn't reply. She gave him a few more bites and then helped him drink. When he was done he leaned his head back against the pillar behind him and closed his eyes.

Annja gathered her things and stood. "If you change your mind," she said, looking down at his sunburned face, "ask for Annja."

No one else is going to stick their neck out for you, that's for sure.

21

It was well after dark when she climbed back up the ridge, another bottle of Gatorade and a rehydrated meal in one hand, her flashlight in the other.

She was expecting to be stopped by whoever had sentry duty at this point, but she reached the ruins without anyone calling out to her. It was dark.

They're just keeping a low profile, she told herself. Don't want to give away their position.

But it was more than that, as she discovered moments later when she reached the place where the prisoner had been secured. No one was there.

Had they done something to him? She paused. Maybe he'd escaped. Annja didn't think he'd managed to get free. If he had, surely his hands would have been left on the ground. Someone had come to get him.

Grimes.

Annja quickly turned around and headed down the ridgeline to the camp below. She made her way through the tents until she came to the larger one. There was a guard stationed outside—Gardner, the scout from the night before—but he waved her inside without a word.

Grimes and Connolly were bent over the camp table. A large-scale topographical map of the surrounding area was spread out before them.

They were discussing the expedition's next target. Several red X's were marked on the map, presumably locations they had either selected for themselves or obtained from Ephraim.

The prisoner wasn't anywhere in sight.

Connolly noticed her first. "Ah, Annja!" he said, gesturing her forward. "You're just the person we need. We're trying to decide where we're headed next and—"

"Where is he?" Annja interrupted him.

Connolly's head cocked to one side. "I beg your pardon. Where is who?"

"The prisoner."

It was Grimes, rather than Connolly, who answered. "We turned him over to the authorities."

Annja looked at him. "The authorities?"

Grimes nodded. "We reached out by radio earlier and brought them up to speed on the situation. When their two officers arrived, they took statements from us and, based on the strength of those statements, they arrested him. I doubt he'll be troubling us for a long time," he finished with a laugh.

As if on cue, Connolly stepped into the conversation. "Rest assured, Ms. Creed, that I kept your name out of things as best I could. I know how little you like the spotlight outside of your duties as host of that cable show you work for."

"Is there some reason I wasn't informed?"

Grimes's eyes narrowed. "Informed? Why?"

"Oh, I don't know," she said, "maybe for the simple reason that I'm the one he tried to kidnap?"

He laughed, but there wasn't anything pleasant about it. "I'm sorry, Ms. Creed, but you were hired to help translate the scroll and for your expertise in uncovering artifacts. I don't presume to tell you how to do your job. I would appreciate it if you would refrain from telling me how to do mine."

"Has the embassy been informed?" she asked, ignoring him.

Connolly frowned. "The embassy?" He exchanged a look with his second in command.

"Yes, the embassy. An attempt was made to kidnap a U.S. citizen on foreign soil. That's a terrorist act and it makes sense to give the embassy a heads-up. In case they try to grab someone else."

Grimes waved the idea away with a flip of his hand. "You can't be serious. If this was an international plot to harm U.S. citizens, don't you think these so-called terrorists would have gone after Mitchell first? Or do you somehow think that being the host of a cable television show makes you a more likely target than one of the world's richest men?"

"Of course I don't," she replied, doing what she could to hold her temper, "but I don't see—"

"I don't care what you see or don't see, Annja," Grimes cut in over her. "The decision is made and the police have already collected their man, so there seems little point in arguing about it further. Now, if there is anything else?"

Annja recognized a dismissal when she heard one.

22

Grimes had said they were going to be charging the Frenchman, if that was indeed what he was, with kidnapping. How could they do that without some kind of a statement from the person he'd actually tried to kidnap? Namely, herself. Neither Grimes nor Connolly would have been able to answer even the most basic of the investigators' questions. After all, she'd been the only one there when the Frenchman had tried to slap that chloroform-soaked cloth over her face in the moments before the attack on the camp. The other two couldn't even testify to seeing it.

It just didn't add up.

She stopped and bent down, fiddling with the lace of her hiking boot as if it had come undone and needed to be retied. While doing so she angled her body slightly and used the position to glance back in the direction she had come, checking that no one was watching her. Satisfied that they weren't, she set off again, but this time slipped between the tents toward the vehicles parked a short distance beyond.

The camp was only so big—nothing more than just a few tents and the firepit, really. It would be fairly obvious if Grimes was holding the prisoner captive in one of the tents. But it would have been a relatively easy matter for him to take the prisoner out into the desert and get rid of him when no one was paying attention.

The lights from the camp didn't reach this far, but there was enough moonlight for Annja to find the trucks without difficulty. She put a hand on the hood of each vehicle as she passed them, looking for the warmth that might signal that a vehicle had been used recently, but each one was cold. In the moonlight, she didn't see any additional tire tracks that would indicate any of the vehicles had moved since their arrival the day before.

She paused, considering. If Grimes was lying to her, there would be some evidence here, somewhere, of what had happened to their captive. She just had to find it.

She repeated her circuit, but this time she moved from the rear of one vehicle to the next, peering into the cargo compartment of each.

Annja found what she was looking for in the third truck she came to.

In the dim light she could see a large wrapped bundle in the middle of the gear. She reached out and tried the door handle. It was unlocked. She eased the door open with one hand, ready to slap the other over the

interior light to keep from giving herself away, but it
didn't come on. Maybe it was broken.

She reached into the cargo space and touched the
bundle. The smooth, slick surface crackled beneath the
pressure of her hand. The noise sounded incredibly loud
to her in her nervous state, but was one she recognized,
at least. It was the sound of the heavy-duty bubble wrap
they used to secure specimens for shipment. She ran
her hands along the object in first one direction and
then the other, trying to get a sense of how big it was.
It stretched forward beyond her reach, so it was at least
three feet long, possibly more. It was also roughly as
wide around…as a person's shoulders.

You need to be sure.

She called her sword to her and used the tip of the
blade to carefully cut through the wrappings closest to
her. The sword was long, the space limited, and it took
her a few minutes of awkward work before she had managed to cut a large enough gash to peel it back. With her
sword in one hand, she reached out again with the other.

She felt a man's boot and then, as she reached higher,
his leg. Even without a light she was confident that she
had found her missing prisoner.

Grimes had lied about the prisoner's death without
batting an eye. What else might he have lied about?
What else might she have missed?

She released her sword so that she would have two
hands to work with and then spent a moment securing
the bubble wrap back around the corpse's feet as best

she could. In the light of day, it would be obvious someone had tampered with the bundle, but it should pass a casual inspection for the time being. She stepped back and gently eased the rear door closed behind her.

The silence about the camp seemed oppressive, dangerous even, and as she made her way back toward the tents she couldn't seem to shake the feeling that her lack of information was going to get someone else killed.

She needed to know more.

Rather than going back to her tent, she changed direction and crept through the darkness toward Connolly's. The guards were posted on the outer perimeter of the camp and so she was able to get close behind the structure without being seen. Light from somewhere inside cast shadows against the canvas walls and with its help she could tell that there were at least two men inside the tent. She assumed they were still Grimes and Connolly. The voices she heard through the canvas moments later confirmed that.

"Didn't tell us anything worthwhile. We still don't know who they are or what they want."

"Of course, we do!" Connolly scoffed. "They want the staff, just as we do." Annja's eyes narrowed. Staff? "Since we know that, it doesn't really matter who they are."

"I'm not so sure about that. The fact that they went after Creed before the map just doesn't feel right. Why would they do that?"

"Maybe they want that mysterious sword you keep talking about."

Annja stiffened when she heard Connolly mention her sword. She thought she'd been discreet and hadn't realized that anyone had noticed her use of the weapon. Apparently Grimes had.

"I'm not making it up," Grimes said sharply. "I know what I saw!"

Connolly laughed indulgently. "Relax, I'm not suggesting otherwise. The question is what we're going to do about it."

"For now? Nothing other than keep an eye on her. But once we find the staff I suggest you use its power to get her to tell you everything she knows about the sword. Who knows, perhaps you'll come away with two artifacts of interest."

That was the second time they'd mentioned a staff. Annja had no idea what they were talking about, but it seemed obvious at this point that the staff was the real reason behind the expedition. Not once had they mentioned the treasure.

She thought back to her work translating the scrolls. She didn't remember anything about a staff. Had she missed something?

"All right, then. How do you propose we should proceed?"

Grimes's tone was full of confidence as he said, "I think it's time to end this farce. With an enemy on our tail, it's better if we cut to the chase and get the staff.

Put Creed and the professor on figuring out the location mentioned in that stanza. Do not pass Go, do not collect two hundred dollars."

Connolly muttered something Annja didn't catch. Grimes's reply, however, was loud and clear.

"If they get in the way, get rid of them. We can always concoct some story later about an accident if need be."

Annja had heard enough.

23

"Ephraim! Wake up, Ephraim!"

Annja punctuated her words by shaking her colleague by the shoulder.

That brought the older man out of his sleep with a jolt. A look of fear crossed his face before he realized who it was kneeling next to him in the darkness.

"Annja? What are you doing here?"

She quickly covered his mouth with her hand. She leaned in close and whispered, "Shhh," only letting go when she felt him nod in understanding.

Annja heard the rustling of Ephraim's sleeping bag and then a quiet click. The weak light of his portable lamp beneath the covers of his sleeping bag came on. The light allowed them to see each other's face but wouldn't easily be seen outside the tent. This time, his voice was barely above a whisper when he asked, "What's going on? Are we under attack again?"

She shook her head. "No, it's worse." She quickly told him what she had overheard.

Ephraim listened quietly, until she got to the part about the staff. His hand shot out and seized her wrist, gripping it fiercely.

"A staff? You're sure that's what he said?"

"I'm positive. I don't have a clue what he's talking about, though, do you? I don't remember seeing anything about a staff in the scroll."

Ephraim's grip on her wrist eased up, but she could still feel the tension coming off him in waves. He said something under his breath in Hebrew. Annja didn't know what it meant, but the tone told her it wasn't good.

"Talk to me, Ephraim. What is it? What's he referring to?"

Her old friend was quiet for a long time. Annja started to think he hadn't heard her, but at last he said, "Aaron's staff. The Staff of Judea. That has to be it. It must have been the treasure referred to in one of the stanzas."

The Staff of Judea?

At the back of her mind, she remembered a long-forgotten story told to her by the nuns at the orphanage in New Orleans. Something about Moses and his brother Aaron…

Seeing her expression, Ephraim explained. "When the Jewish people were captive in Egypt, the Lord sent Moses and his brother Aaron to confront the pharaoh and demand the release of the Israelites. As a symbol of his authority, God gave them each a staff of miraculous power. Moses's staff had power over the natural elements and he used it to part the Red Sea and draw water from a stone during the Exodus. Aaron's, on the other hand, was much more potent."

Annja looked at him skeptically. "You do realize there's no scientific evidence for the parting of the Red Sea, right?"

Ephraim waved her comment away. "When the brothers confronted the pharaoh, he demanded to see a miracle, so Aaron threw down his staff and it turned into a snake. When the pharaoh's sorcerers duplicated the act with their own staves, Aaron's staff attacked and swallowed them all. When this was still not enough to persuade the pharaoh, Aaron called upon the power of the staff a second time and ushered in the ten plagues of Egypt."

That, at least, was one of the Bible stories she did remember from her childhood. God supposedly sent ten plagues to convince the Egyptian ruler to release the Israelites from bondage. She tried to list them all from memory. There was the water that turned into blood, and then the plagues of frogs, gnats and flies. She remembered those easily enough. After that things got a bit hazy, though. She thought there was something about cows and…boils? Cows with boils, maybe? Those were followed by a plague of thunder and darkness, and finally, the ultimate plague, the death of the firstborn.

"Later," Ephraim went on, "after Jerusalem was restored, the staff was used by the Davidic kings as a scepter and stored in the temple. Legend has it that the staff miraculously vanished from the temple hours before it was destroyed."

"Just like the treasure," Annja replied and Ephraim nodded his head.

They knew what had happened to the treasure—that much of the story, at least, was true. So perhaps the legend of the staff was, as well. Being the bearer of a mystical weapon herself made it that much more difficult for her to dismiss the possibility outright. And if the staff did indeed exist, then perhaps there was some truth to the rest of the story.

A man like Connolly with the power to call down the plagues of Egypt on any city he chose? Annja shivered and it wasn't because of the night air.

Ephraim stared at her and Annja could see the naked fear on his face even as he said, "We cannot allow the staff to fall into Connolly's hands, no matter what."

"Agreed." She nodded. "Right now, though, we need to get you and the rest of the team out of here."

Her old friend wasn't so easily swayed. "How are you going to do that? You're just one woman, Annja."

One woman, yes, but one woman with a very special sword.

"I'll handle it. Don't worry." A plan was already forming in her mind. She would get the iPad with the translated verses away from Connolly and then use it to find the staff herself. Once she had, she'd turn it over to Roux for him to safeguard. They'd done so with other dangerous artifacts in the past. Short of destroying it, something she could never bring herself to do, it seemed the best option. She didn't entirely trust Roux—he had his own agenda, there was no doubt about that—but she was confident that he wouldn't suddenly go berserk and try to destroy some national capital simply out of spite.

Connolly, on the other hand, would.

Ephraim finally turned to pack his things. "Unless it's extremely personal," Annja told him, "just leave it. We don't have time to secure all the gear and leaving it in place might help disguise that you're gone until the last possible moment. The bigger head start you get, the better."

The plan was simple and Annja took a moment to lay it out for Ephraim. He would be in charge of getting his students ready to go. While he was doing that, she would sneak around to the far side of camp and create a diversion, drawing the security team in her direction. With the team distracted, Ephraim would load everyone into the nearest vehicle and head for the closest city while she circled back around to Connolly's tent to steal the iPad containing the scroll translations. Once she had them, she would escape the same way Ephraim had, in another stolen Land Cruiser.

She tried not to think about the fact that by that point the security team wouldn't hesitate to riddle her with bullets if they caught her in the act. And that they'd be ready for her this time.

Ephraim was already dressed so all he had to do was pull on his boots. When he was finished, Annja said,

"Remember, we need to look like everything's fine. We're just two friends out for a casual walk, nothing to be worried or concerned about. Look as normal as you can."

As they left the tent, Ephraim began regaling her with memories of a dig he'd recently conducted in Laodicea. Annja played along, laughing and asking questions in the right places. When they reached the tent shared by the other two women, they said good-night and went their separate ways—Ephraim slipping inside to talk to the others while Annja headed off into the darkness at the edge of camp where they had dug a pit latrine earlier that afternoon.

She paused in the darkness, waited a few minutes to be certain she was alone and that she hadn't been followed, then quickly changed direction and headed back toward where the vehicles were parked. She needed a diversion, one big enough to attract the attention of everyone in the camp. After a moment's hard thinking, she had the answer.

24

After the surprise attack the night before, Grimes had set up roving patrols and ordered that two men be patrolling the camp perimeter on a rotating schedule all night long. This was both a blessing and a curse, in Annja's view. It would give her time to gather what she needed from the parked vehicles once she was sure the patrol had already passed by. But it also made moving in the darkness that much more difficult because she couldn't know where the patrol was at any given time.

She approached the parked vehicles openly and at an unhurried pace. She had a story ready should she need it; the lantern in her tent had run out of batteries and she needed some new ones. Since she had helped direct how the supplies were loaded onto the trucks, she knew batteries could be found in most of the vehicles and therefore it was a safe bet as an excuse. It would be far more dangerous once she had what she had come for, but that couldn't be helped. If she was stopped at that point, she would have no choice but to fight her way out.

Thankfully the guards were elsewhere at the moment and Annja was quickly able to find what she needed. Duffel bag in hand, she locked the door, closed it and turned around.

"Identify yourself!" a man called out from the darkness, freezing her in place. Gardner appeared seconds later, his gun in hand and pointed at her.

"Don't shoot," she said playfully, doing her utmost to appear calm all she wanted to do was run before it was too late.

Gardner looked over her shoulder at the vehicle and then down at the bag in her hands before he dropped the barrel of his gun. He didn't put it away, but at least it wasn't pointing directly at her anymore. Something about his stance and his no-nonsense attitude told her he wouldn't hesitate to use it against her should the need arise.

"What are you doing out here?" he asked.

No one needed a duffel bag to carry a few batteries. Time for plan B.

"One of the GPR units was giving us trouble this afternoon, so I'm going to switch out the pulse-induction units with these spares and see if that solves the problem."

The ground-penetrating radar devices were some of the most important equipment they had brought with them on the expedition. Designed to send strong pulses of radar waves deep beneath the ground, they allowed the team to see what might be buried beneath the surface without lifting the first shovelful of dirt. The devices were also rather temperamental, a fact everyone on the dig knew at this point. Annja did her best to affect an air of annoyance at the trouble the devices were supposedly giving her and prayed that Gardner wouldn't ask to look in the bags.

"Do you want me to carry that for you?" he asked.

The question was so unexpected that for a moment Annja couldn't make heads or tails of it. *Carry* that? *Carry* what? And then she realized that he was talking about the duffel bag supposedly holding the spare pulse-induction units.

Was he trying to trick me? she wondered.

As he waited for her answer, Gardner smiled tentatively.

That's when she got it. Gardner was sweet on her! And here she'd thought he was ready to blow her brains out. Could she be wrong about this? When he'd guarded the prisoner, he'd seemed to her to be the security team member who most had it in for her....

"Oh, no thanks," she said. "I can handle this."

But he wouldn't be denied that easily.

"No reason you should have to carry the bag when I'm perfectly willing."

Annja shook her head. "I couldn't pull you away from your duty, Gardner. What would Grimes do if he found out?"

She realized her mistake the moment she said it. She'd just unintentionally thrown down the gauntlet, for if he backed out now he would look like he was afraid of Grimes.

"No, please," he said more forcefully. "I insist." He slung his weapon over his shoulder and reached out.

It took every ounce of Annja's willpower not to pull back away from him.

"Sure," she said, her heart hammering in her throat as she passed over the bag.

"Hey, these aren't so heavy," he said, hefting the bag up and down a few inches.

Gardner didn't seem to notice the sounds of banging inside the bag. "Heavy, no, but they *are* very delicate. Be careful please."

"Oops, sorry," he said. "My bad."

He moved his arm outward a few inches, holding the bag away from his body so that it wouldn't bump against the side of his leg.

"Better?"

"Yes. Thank you." Her heart felt like it was going to explode, it was beating so fast.

"So where are we taking it?"

Not wanting to say "her tent" and give him any ideas, she thought quickly. "Ephraim and I will be working on it in his tent, with the help of some of the students."

"Okay. Sounds good."

They were almost to the tent when the radio on Gardner's belt crackled into life.

"Command to Eagle One."

Gardner carefully passed the bag back to Annja before pulling the radio from his belt.

"Eagle One here. Go, Command," he said, then inclined his head back in the direction of his patrol route, indicating that he was headed off.

Annja mouthed a quick "thank you" to him and then he was striding briskly away and she was breathing a major sigh of relief.

She waited until she couldn't hear his radio any longer, then glanced about. Satisfied, she hefted the bag and quickly started walking on a diagonal course away from camp.

It was pretty dark, the thin sliver of moon barely providing enough light for her to see where to put her feet, but she wasn't complaining. If she couldn't see where she was going, the sentries would have an equally hard time seeing her.

She walked about a hundred yards away from camp and then began looking for a good spot to set up. A long, flat table of rock that was roughly waist high seemed to be the best bet, so she clambered up. Unzipping the bag, she sorted through the items by feel, setting them in a semicircle around her on the rock. After that, it was simply a matter of putting it all together.

She put her flashlight inside the bag and turned it on, muting most of the light. She took a blasting cap out of the bag and put it on the rock in front of her. It was a very small charge, used in excavation work to break apart rocks that were just too big to move by hand, and would do nicely for what she had in mind. She attached a detonation cord to the blast cap and then ran the cord to the timer. She set the timer for ten minutes.

Next she took the boxes of spare ammunition out of the duffel, opened them and one by one poured their contents on top of the blasting cap until it was buried under a veritable pile of ammunition intended for the security team's MP4s. The pièce de résistance was the three boxes of shells for a combat shotgun.

She stopped and surveyed her handiwork. It looked good; when the blasting cap was triggered it should cook off some of the ammunition directly on top of it, which would then cause the rest of the pile to go off, as well. Within seconds it would sound like there was a full-scale war going on as round after round went off. As long as it gave Ephraim and his charges enough time to escape.

One last check to be sure the det cord was connected properly to the timer and then she set the countdown for ten minutes, hit the switch and got the heck out of there.

25

It took her seven minutes to reach the tent they'd chosen as their rendezvous point. She hadn't seen nor heard anyone on her way back; the rest of the camp seemed to have settled in for the night.

She slipped inside to find Ephraim waiting with the rest of their group.

"All right," she said softly. "Everyone know the drill?"

There were nods all around.

Annja checked her watch. "In about three minutes you're going to hear a lot of noise. Don't worry. It's nothing that can hurt you. As soon as you hear it, though, I want you all to head across camp to where the Land Cruisers are parked. Take the last one in line. The keys are above the visor."

"What about you? How are you going to get out?" Susan asked.

"I'll be about five minutes behind you in one of the other vehicles, don't worry."

"Why don't you just come with us now?" Rachel said, but Annja shook her head.

"Someone needs to draw them off your tail and I've got the best chance of pulling it off. You guys stay close to Ephraim and I'll see you all shortly."

Gunfire suddenly split the night air, the shots coming fast and furious. To Annja it sounded like half a dozen people had suddenly started blazing away with everything they had and she smiled at the sound.

Tony was waiting at the front of the tent. His keen eyes and reflexes would serve them better than Ephraim's as they navigated away from camp and so he was the first out the door. Annja tapped him on the shoulder and said, "Go!"

The others followed behind him in a steady stream until it was only Annja and Ephraim left inside the tent. He gave her a swift hug, then gripped her shoulders tightly.

"I've changed my mind," he said. "It's too dangerous. Leave the map and come with us. We can worry about the staff later."

But Annja shook her head. "This is our one and only chance. You know it as well as I do. The minute Connolly gets his hands on the staff, it will disappear into his personal collection, secure behind an army of armed guards and modern alarm systems. No, our only chance is to beat him to it."

Shouts could be heard outside now as the security team responded to what they must have thought was a major attack. They didn't have much time. "I'll be fine," she said. "Go. Now!"

"All right, all right." But instead of leaving, he dug into his pocket, pulled out a few folded sheets of paper and thrust them into Annja's hands. "Here, take this," he said. "You're going to need it."

"What is it?"

"Legend says the staff is secure inside the walls of the Fortress Mal'akh. While you were gone I wrote down everything I could remember about the legend. Along with the translated verse, this might help if you get there first."

Ephraim's insight was priceless and she knew the information he provided would be extremely useful, provided they managed to get out of here intact.

A chance that was growing slimmer every second they stood here.

"Thank you. Truly. Now get out of here and get those students of yours to safety!"

"Right!" he said. "Good luck." And then he pushed out of the tent and into the night.

Annja gave him a moment and then she followed suit. She slipped between the tents, heading for the one shared by Grimes and Connolly. She could hear the gunfire still going off in the distance, though now it was answered by the sharp crack of shots from several MP4s. She smiled. It meant that Grimes's security team was still chasing down her little decoy.

Who knew you could have so much fun with a blasting cap and half a dozen boxes of ammunition?

She heard the sound of a car engine start up and knew Ephraim had reached the others. Cautiously she approached her employer's tent.

The lanterns were on and the flaps thrown back, giving her a good look inside. It seemed to be empty. She glanced around, sensing the trap but not seeing anything concrete to move her suspicions in one direction or the other.

Where were they?

Does it matter? her conscience asked.

No, probably not.

She slipped inside and headed directly for the steamer trunk she had seen Connolly remove the iPad from the night before. She reached to open the lid, only to find it was locked.

Good thing I brought the key, she thought, and called her sword from the otherwhere. She slid the tip of the weapon into the seam where the lid met the chest and then pushed down sharply.

It popped open on the first try and she let her sword vanish again.

She dug through the contents, throwing aside what she wasn't interested in, until she found the leather iPad case. She unzipped it, checked to make sure the device was inside and then closed it again.

Annja stood, turned around…and found herself staring down the barrel of a gun for the second time in less than a week.

Martin Grimes was holding the gun.

"Going somewhere, Ms. Creed?" he asked with a very satisfied expression on his face.

Just like that she knew beyond a shadow of a doubt that the gunman at the Shrine of the Book had been none other than Grimes.

Her expression must have given her away. He suddenly chuckled. "Figured it out, have you? Took you bloody long enough. I thought you were supposed to be smart, Creed."

He laughed, throwing his head back slightly as he did so.

That was all Annja needed.

She pulled her arm back and whipped it forward again, the motion reminiscent of an Olympic javelin thrower. Her sword materialized in her hand before it had even half completed its arc and the force of her throw sent it hurtling point first directly at Grimes. As soon as the sword had left her grip, Annja threw herself to the side, using her body to cushion the iPad as she crashed to the floor.

Grimes's gun boomed.

Two quick shots in rapid succession.

The first missed Annja by scant inches as she dove to the side, the slug disappearing through the fabric of the tent.

The second bullet skimmed the edge of the blade

as it hurtled toward him, changing the trajectory slightly. As a result, the broadsword slammed point first into Grimes's right shoulder rather than piercing him through the spot Annja had been aiming for—the center of his chest.

Grimes went over backward, screaming, the gun flying out of his hand to land halfway between him and Annja.

She scrambled to her feet and called her sword to hand, the weapon disappearing from Grimes's shoulder and reappearing in her grip as she crossed the room at a dead run. She kicked Grimes's gun into the shadows, then moved around him in a wide circle, intent on reaching the entrance. He barely noticed, too busy trying to staunch the flow of blood from his wound.

Annja burst out of the entrance and nearly ran over Hamilton and Beck as they raced to respond to the sound of the pistol shots from inside the tent. Annja knew how she must look, with a bloody sword in one hand and Connolly's leather iPad case in the other, but she didn't even stop. Instead, she pointed back of her shoulder and shouted, "Hurry! Grimes is holding them off so I can get this—" she held up the case "—to Mr. Connolly but he's not going to last much longer on his own! He needs help!"

For a second she didn't think they were going to believe her. Beck, in particular, had a curious expression on his face, as if he were trying to work out what was wrong with the picture she was presenting, but then Hamilton was racing to Connolly's tent and Beck moved to follow him.

Her victory was short-lived, however.

She hadn't taken another ten steps before a line of semiautomatic fire stitched itself through the earth near her feet and Grimes's voice filled the night.

"Kill her!" he screamed.

26

Annja jigged to the right behind a pair of tents, taking her out of Grimes's line of sight, but the damage was done. Anyone in earshot would know something was wrong, and since they were all Grimes's men, they were more likely to shoot first and ask questions later.

She had to get to the vehicles!

Unfortunately, she couldn't outrun the radios Grimes and his men all carried.

By the time she reached the edge of camp where the SUVs were parked, Grimes had used the radio to let the others know that Annja was persona non grata and to shoot her on sight. She knew this because that was exactly what they tried to do as she came running toward the parked vehicles.

Bullets split the night around her, one coming so close she felt it move her hair, and then she was on the ground and rolling, trying to get out of the line of fire. She fetched up against a fair-size boulder and scrambled behind it, squatting down low and trying to catch her breath.

The gunfire continued, the bullets slashing through the darkness around her, but none of them came close. The gunmen couldn't see her anymore, so most of the shots were wild, though one or two ricocheted off the stone she was hiding behind.

She had to get out of here, behind the wheel of one of the Land Cruisers. It would take her days to walk to the nearest town and she didn't have food or water. Besides, she'd be overtaken by Connolly's men that way.

Grimes, of course, would know that. Which was why he was no doubt stationing his men near the trucks.

She was about to realize that Grimes wasn't content to wait for her.

One minute Annja was curled up tight behind a rock, hidden from view, and then the area in which she was hiding was lit up as bright as day by two SUVs, pinning her in place.

"You've got ten seconds to come out or I'm going to send my men in there with guns blazing, Creed," Grimes shouted. He paused, and then said, "Do us all a favor and stay hidden, will you? It will be so much more fun that way!"

"Ten…"

She glanced around frantically, looking for a way out.

"Nine…"

She could guess what Grimes would do to her if he managed to capture her.

"Eight…"

No, she needed to move, but had to do it in such a way that she stayed out of sight.

"Seven…"

The light had revealed that the rock she was hiding behind was bigger than she thought when she rolled up against it in the darkness. That was good, because right about now it was the only thing between her and Grimes's men. But the minute she came out from behind it…

"Six…"

Unless…

The ground directly in front of where she was hiding ran straight for about twenty yards before it dipped sharply out of sight. She had no idea what was beyond that point—it could be an abrupt hundred-foot drop for all she knew—but right now it was about the only option open to her. If she took off running in any other direction she wouldn't get ten steps before being riddled with bullets. At least this way she might have a chance.

Might.

"Five-four-three-two-one! Time's up. Here we come…."

She heard the engines race behind her and saw the lights shift position as the vehicles headed in her direction.

It was now or never.

Annja took a firm grip on the iPad case, breathed deeply to hyperoxygenate her blood supply and then took off running in a straight line directly away from the boulder she'd been using for cover.

She made the first five yards without being seen. The ground beneath her feet was smooth and level, the footing even, and she was able to pour on the speed after her initial burst out of the gate.

Behind her she could hear the roar of the trucks and the shouts of Grimes and his men as they taunted her with what was to come. She kept her head down and ran.

By the time she hit the halfway point, however, her luck ran out. The floodlights of one of the vehicles caught her as she leaped over a rock in the middle of the trail and seconds later bullets stitched a path right past her left side as she deked in the opposite direction.

"There she is! Over there!"

The SUVs swerved to keep her in sight and more gunfire followed. She was closing in on some larger boulders that might provide cover, but for now all she could do was duck and swoop from side to side in an effort to escape the bullets.

Pain flared along her right biceps as a bullet creased her skin, causing her to stumble. The motion actually saved her life as the gunner put several more rounds through the space she would have been if she hadn't faltered. She caught herself against a nearby rock before pushing off and charging in the opposite direction even as the surface of the rock was riddled with hot lead.

Her legs were burning, her heart was pounding, but she pushed on, repeating a phrase like a mantra in her mind.

Stop and die. Move and live.

Stop and die. Move and live.

She ducked around a nearby boulder just as a bullet sent rock chips flying into her unprotected face, lacerating her cheek and right ear. She barely noticed, her attention centered on the drop looming directly ahead of her.

Thanks to the floodlights behind her, Annja could see that the path she was following disappeared into darkness on the other side of the dip and she clenched her teeth as the enemy closed in from behind.

The trucks behind her had to swerve to avoid the boulder field she was moving through now and for a moment she ran out of the light.

She raced forward, reached the drop and continued down in a partially controlled slip-and-slide, kicking out chunks of loose earth and stone from the slope as she fought to keep herself upright and moving.

If she stumbled now it would be over. If the fall didn't kill her, Grimes's men would.

She heard the trucks stop somewhere above her and voices carried down the slope as doors slammed and men shouted for flashlights.

She'd gained a few seconds, but not much more.

With a jolt she found herself at the bottom of the slope. From what little moonlight there was, she could see that she had come down onto a wide, even path about the same width as a road. At first she had no idea what it was, but then she understood that she was standing in a dry riverbed, the sand packed solid beneath her feet.

She didn't think, just trusted her gut and took off to the left. A glance over her shoulder showed them coming down the slope after her, their flashlights bobbing in the darkness.

She could hear her breath rasping in and out of her lungs. If she didn't find some way of losing them in the dark in the next several minutes she was going to run out of...

A sound intruded on her consciousness, a low rumble that seemed to be steadily growing in volume as if something was closing in on her. In seconds the sound was loud enough to drown out the shouts and jeers of the men chasing her. Annja had a sudden vision of a flash flood racing around the bend behind her, but dismissed the notion as crazy. There had to be rain for there to be a flash flood and the region had been bone-dry for weeks.

She chanced a glance behind her but didn't see anything. The rumble grew louder.

The ground beneath her feet was shaking. Twice she stumbled and almost went down. Whatever it was, it was very close now.

Another glance back and this time she could see dark forms on horseback charging toward her. What looked like giant wings spread out behind them.

The first rider passed her on the left, the second on the right. She had a moment to notice the dark, desert clothes they were wearing and then the third rider burst out of the shadows behind her.

One minute she was charging forward, the next a muscled arm swooped around her waist and lifted her off the ground, her legs still churning uselessly beneath her.

27

For a moment Annja fought against the arm of the man who held her, but the idea of falling beneath the hooves of the horse held little appeal. She stopped and swung her leg up and over the horse's neck so that she was now seated in front of the rider. She dug her fingers into the horse's mane and held on.

The group burst out of the riverbed and onto a flat plain stretching ahead of them as far as Annja could see. Which wasn't far given the limited moonlight, but she had the sense of vast openness. The horsemen spread out into a wide arc on either side of Annja's rescuer, and she could see that there were at least a dozen, maybe more. They were dressed just as the Bedouin pretenders had been, in black desert garments that covered them from head to toe. Only the strip around their eyes had been left free, the rest of their faces covered by their kuffiyas, protecting them from the flying sand and hiding their features at the same time. The horses' hooves thundered against the earth as they charged forward.

"Where are you taking me?" Annja shouted in French.

The man glanced at her, but didn't say anything.

A burst of gunfire whizzed over their heads and the lights of a moving vehicle splashed across the group.

Annja glanced over her rescuer's shoulder and saw one of Grimes's Land Cruisers in their wake. They must have come down the ridgeline by the path they'd originally taken to get to the dig and then cut across country to flank Annja. It was a good plan and they'd only failed because Annja was no longer on foot.

Without a word, the riders split into two packs. Half of them closed ranks and cut to the left, charging diagonally away from the pursuing vehicle, while the other half, including Annja, did the same in the opposite direction. The other riders with them closed up ranks around Annja, doing what they could to shield her from being noticed.

The driver of the SUV continued directly ahead, apparently undecided about which group to pursue.

The other way, Annja thought fiercely, go the other way.

The Land Cruiser jerked right and headed after the group containing Annja.

"Can't a girl catch a break?" she said aloud, which, to her surprise, elicited a chuckle from her rescuer.

A hail of bullets cut short her realization that he spoke English. The rider leaned forward in an attempt to reduce wind resistance, forcing Annja to do the same.

The smell of horse filled her nostrils as she bent over its neck. She could hear other guns and realized that her rescuers were firing back.

Bullets cracked and whined around them. Annja watched as the rider to their left was toppled from his saddle. The man's horse charged forward, surged ahead of Annja, relieved of the extra weight in the wake of its rider's demise.

Grimes's men were leaning on the horn, trying to spook the horses, but these mounts must have been exceptionally well trained. They responded to the riders' commands with just the slightest touch.

A crash of glass reached Annja's ears and some of the lights behind them went out. More shots were fired, another rider slipped from the saddle and then darkness fell once more as the headlights and floodlamps of the SUV were extinguished with several carefully placed shots.

Instantly the pack divided once more, the riders breaking off onto individual paths, splitting up and again offering multiple targets. Annja was amazed at their coordination. That kind of synchronicity didn't happen by chance. Whoever these men were, they had ridden together for some time.

She was still pondering that when the unthinkable happened. A stray bullet caught their horse in the side of the chest. It stumbled and then abruptly collapsed beneath them, flinging Annja and the rider from its back like stones from a sling.

Annja felt herself flying through the air for a second before she hit the ground hard, bounced once and rapped her head against a nearby rock. She was unconscious before she fully understood what had happened.

ANNJA AWOKE TO FIND herself lying on a cot inside a large safari tent. She blinked several times, trying to figure out what she was seeing, and then sat up abruptly when she remembered being flung from the horse in the middle of the gunfight.

That was a mistake. The pain pulsed inside her head like a living thing. She closed her eyes and held her head in her hands as she waited for the pain to pass. It took a long time and her stomach was queasy afterward, which told her she'd best take it easy for a few days until she could be sure she didn't have a concussion.

Of course, a concussion was the least of her worries if she'd been captured by Grimes and Connolly.

The fact that she was lying on a clean bunk inside a tent gave her hope. The light in the tent let her know the night had passed. From the look of it, it was at least mid-afternoon, if not later.

She was dressed in the clothing she'd been wearing the night before, but the cuts on her hands and face had been cleaned and treated. A stiffness around her right biceps let her know that the bullet wound there had been cleaned and swathed in bandages, as well.

She got up off the cot slowly, discovering as she put her feet on the floor that she was still wearing her boots. That was something else to be thankful for, as she never would have been able to pull them on by herself the way she was feeling.

Once she was up, it was a matter of walking forward until she reached the entrance to the tent. She steeled herself for what she might see, then stuck her head out the door.

She was in the midst of a simple desert camp. A smaller tent stood next to the one she was in and between them was a smoldering fire. An iron rack had been set up over the fire and several pots were resting on it, the smell of a meal emanating from them. A table stood nearby and a long-legged, silver-haired man was seated there, food laid out before him. He must have heard her because he turned and smiled when he saw her standing in the doorway of the tent.

"Hello, Annja," Roux said.

28

Annja stared at Roux for a long moment and then crossed the distance between them and slapped him hard across the face.

Roux didn't move, though the smile on his face faltered just a little. "I guess I deserve that."

"You guess?" Annja grated, having a hard time restraining herself from slapping him again.

"Now, Annja, let's discuss this calmly, please."

His placating tone fired her up further. "You want to discuss this calmly? After you sent armed gunmen to kidnap me and attack my camp? Are you out of your mind?"

The fact that the so-called Bedouins had spoken French had been her first clue. The rest had just been educated guesswork, until now.

"I had good reasons, Annja, and if you'd stop shouting for five minutes perhaps I'd have the opportunity to explain. Now sit down."

That last was delivered with a tone of command and

Annja found herself responding to it almost before she realized it. She threw herself into one of the chairs at the table and glared at him.

"That's better," he said. "Would you like something to eat?" He gestured at the table where there was a platter of stuffed Cornish hens, as well as bowls of fruit and vegetables. Annja suddenly realized she hadn't eaten since dinner the night before. The food smelled so good that she decided it would be foolish to let it go to waste. As she served herself, Roux began to talk.

"I left for Monte Carlo shortly after we parted on Tuesday and didn't realize that you'd signed on to help Connolly in his quest to solve the riddle of the scroll. As soon as I learned you had, I immediately returned to Jerusalem."

Annja let the issue of how he'd found out she'd joined Connolly's expedition go by without protest. She'd known Roux long enough to know that he had a global network of information providers that outrivaled that of the CIA and MI6 combined. He'd kept tabs on her in the past and she wasn't surprised to hear he'd done the same now. What did surprise her was the speed at which he'd returned to the Holy Land and gotten involved in the search for the treasure.

"You could have just called me, you know."

Roux shook his head. "Actually, I couldn't. I believe your phone is being monitored."

Annja stared at him. "Run that by me again?"

"Your phone isn't safe. I believe Connolly's chief

of staff has been monitoring it since you left the city. He's an extremely dangerous man, Annja, as is his boss. They're after something more than this ridiculous treasure."

"I know. He's after Aaron's staff. The Staff of Judea."

Now it was Roux's turn to stare. "You know about the staff?"

"Up until a few hours ago, I would have said no. But I'm a quick learner." She told him about the events that had led her to eavesdrop on Connolly and Grimes and what she had subsequently learned from Ephraim about the staff.

Roux let out a long streak of curse words, some of which were rather creative. Then again, after living for five hundred years traditional swear words probably wouldn't satisfy her anymore, either, she thought wryly. She waited for him to finish and then said, "I take it you believe the staff is real."

Roux cast her a withering glance. "Of course it's real. Artifacts with true power such as this one are few and far between."

Annja poured herself a glass of cool water and took a long drink. Her encounter in the desert had left her parched.

"So, let me see if I have this straight." She put her glass back down on the table, afraid of what she might do with it if it was still in hand by the time she was finished. "You needed to reach me, but were concerned that my phone was tapped. So instead, you came up with the bright idea of sending Parisian mercenaries dressed up as Bedouin raiders to the camp to scare us off. And when that didn't work, you ordered the same group to kidnap me right out from under everyone else's noses."

Roux ignored her rising tone, something he seemed to be quite good at, and asked, "How did you know they were Parisian mercenaries?"

Annja stared at him for a moment and then ticked several points off with her fingers. "Parisian accent, for one. Military surplus boots, for another. Lack of a decent tan but familiarity with Bedouin customs suggested former service with the French Foreign Legion, for a third. That's off the top of my head."

"I see," he replied, frowning.

If there was one thing Roux hated, it was being upstaged. Annja knew he was irked that she'd worked it out so quickly.

A sudden thought occurred to her.

"Roux?"

"Umm?" he answered, distracted.

"Where are all your people?"

He focused on her again. "People? There's no one here but me and Henshaw."

Henshaw was Roux's combination majordomo, butler and bodyguard. Annja had known him nearly as long as she had known Roux and always found the big man's presence reassuring.

"That's not what I meant. Where are the rest of your

fake Bedouins? Do they have another camp of their own?"

Roux gave her an odd look. "My Bedouins, as you call them, are dead, Annja. You said so yourself. Connolly's men killed them."

She shook her head. "No, your *other* men. The ones who rescued me last night?"

Roux shrugged. "I'm not sure what to tell you, Annja. It was chance that Henshaw stumbled upon you last night while en route to my location. You were wandering in the desert, with a wound to your head and a leather case clutched in one hand like a life preserver."

"Wandering in the desert? That…doesn't make any sense." She hadn't imagined those horsemen and she certainly wouldn't have escaped from Grimes's security force without their help. Who on earth were they? And what had happened after that horse had been shot out from under her?

"The case," she said. "Where is it?"

"Henshaw."

A moment later the tall British-trained butler Annja had first met at Roux's Paris estate stuck his head out of the other tent. "Sir?"

"Bring me that device Annja had with her last night."

"Of course, sir."

Henshaw disappeared back into his tent, only to emerge moments later with the iPad she'd fought so hard to protect. As he drew closer, Annja could see the cracks in the faceplate of the device, but it wasn't until he actually handed it to her that she saw the full extent of the damage.

There was a bullet-hole right through the center of the device.

"Damn."

It was like a blow to the chest. She'd done everything she could to protect it during her mad dash into the desert, all of which had apparently been a complete waste of time and energy. For all she knew it hadn't survived the first volley of gunfire leveled at her.

"I suppose there's no chance of recovering the data stored on the drive?" she asked Henshaw, whose knowledge of electronics outdistanced her own.

He shook his head. "There might be, but I don't have the necessary equipment here to do it."

"Something important, I take it?" Roux asked.

"Oh, nothing much, really. Just the clues leading to the staff's hiding place. I'm sure we can do without those, right?"

Ignoring her sarcasm, Roux got up from the table, disappeared inside his tent and emerged a few minutes later with a few pieces of paper. "Will these help?" he asked.

Annja recognized them right away. "Ephraim's notes!" she said, snatching them out of his hand in her excitement. "Where did you get these?"

"You had them in your pocket when Henshaw found you in the desert. I couldn't make heads or tails of them."

Annja hadn't had time to examine them when Ephraim had given them to her, so she had no idea what Roux was talking about until she unfolded the pages.

They weren't written in any language she was familiar with.

"What the heck?"

Roux smiled. "That's what I was hoping you could tell me."

Annja puzzled over it for a few minutes. As strange as it looked, it also seemed tantalizingly familiar, as if the language was very close to English....

When she figured it out, she laughed aloud.

"Perhaps you could fill me in on what's so amusing?' Roux asked. He really hated being the one not in the know.

"Do you have a mirror?" she asked.

Roux glanced at Henshaw, who disappeared back into his tent and returned a few moments later with a handheld shaving mirror. Roux took it from him.

"Hold it upright where we can see it," she told him. Once he had, she held up one of the pages next to it so that the writing on the page was reflected in the surface of the mirror.

"Bah, it's still gibberish."

Annja took a peek, saw that it was and quickly flipped the page over so that she was holding it upside down. The writing in the mirror transformed into perfectly readable English.

In order to keep a casual observer from understanding what he had written, Ephraim had written his message upside down and backward. It was a clever trick and one that didn't take too much time or effort to learn to do well. Somewhere in his past, Ephraim had clearly made use of the code before.

"Let's see what Ephraim had to tell us, shall we?"

Roux began taking notes as Annja read the pages off to him.

29

"So now what?" Connolly asked.

He and Grimes were sitting outside their tent, quietly discussing the events of the night before over Scotch. The search for the staff had not gone well—had not really even begun—and the blame for that could be put firmly at the feet of one person: Annja Creed.

"I don't see any reason for us not to continue," his chief of security and closest confidant responded.

Connolly frowned. "You don't think she'll go right to the authorities?"

Grimes shook his head. "No, I don't. If that had been her plan, she never would have stayed behind for the iPad. No, she's after bigger game."

"The treasure?"

"No, I think she's after the staff."

That got Connolly's attention. "The staff? What on earth gives you that idea?"

Grimes turned and looked at his boss. He'd been with the man for almost fifteen years and if there was one thing he had learned it was that Connolly was great at the bigger-vision stuff but sometimes he was terribly deficient when it came to connecting the dots at the micro level.

"Think about it," Grimes said. "If she just wanted the cash all she had to do was stay with the expedition and take her share of the finder's fee when the time came. All aboveboard and legal. With the kind of money we're talking about here, she would have been richer than she ever imagined. To you, it's peanuts. But to someone like her? No, she's after the staff."

Connolly waved the idea away. "First of all, how does she even know about it? And second, what on earth would she do with it?"

Grimes laughed. "Who cares what she'd do with it? That's beside the point. This woman made her career chasing down artifacts just like this. Do you really think she'd pass up the chance to be the one to discover the staff Aaron used to call down the plagues of Egypt?"

"No, I don't imagine she would," his employer answered after a moment's consideration.

"Exactly. Neither do I. Which is why we have to get there first. And I know just how to do it. Let's go see if our guest is ready to talk, shall we?"

They crossed the camp to where a new, large canvas tent had been erected. Johnson and Daniels stood guard outside.

"Any problems?" Grimes asked.

"Quiet as a mouse," Daniels replied.

The smile Grimes flashed in response was far from pleasant. "Let's see if we can make him more talkative then, shall we?"

The three men stepped inside the tent, leaving Johnson to stand guard outside. The encounter in the desert last night had been more a massacre than a firefight. They had taken twenty shots for every one the men on horseback had managed. It was only by sheer luck that any of the horsemen had escaped. If Beck's truck hadn't blown a tire at an inopportune moment, they probably would have slaughtered them to a man. As it was, only a few of them had gotten away.

Unfortunately, one of those who'd escaped had been carrying Annja.

No matter, he thought, we've got everything we need right here.

A portable hoist, the kind the archaeologists had brought along to remove heavy rocks or, if they got lucky enough, loads of treasure, out of the earth stood in the center of the tent.

Hanging from it was Professor Ephraim Yellin.

The cords that had been used to tie his hands together had been looped over the hook at the center of the hoist and then the hoist had been cranked up to its highest setting. Ephraim's feet, also bound together, were left hanging about an inch off the floor. It wasn't much, just a small distance, really. If he stretched himself to the limit he could touch the toes of his shoes to the floor and take a little of the weight off his arms for a moment or two. But he couldn't hold the position for long. His arms and legs would start trembling. That in turn would set his body to rotating slightly on the hook above his head, and he'd be right back to where he was, hanging with all his weight on his arms. If left in that position, he'd eventually suffocate as the muscles in his chest failed from the strain.

Grimes expected him to break long before that point.

Beck had needed to let off a little steam so Grimes had allowed him to work the old man over and it showed. The professor's face had taken a beating; one eye was swollen completely shut, the nose looked broken and at least two teeth were missing.

It was really too bad, Grimes thought. The professor could have saved himself a lot of trouble by cooperating.

Grimes stepped around in front of Ephraim. The old man's head was hanging down against his chest, but Grimes noted with satisfaction that the prisoner was still conscious. Ephraim tracked Grimes's movement with his one good eye.

"This doesn't have to continue, you know, Professor," Grimes told him. "Simply agree to do what we ask and we'll have you down from there in a jiff. What do you say?"

There was a moment of silence as the professor worked his lips.

Grimes leaned closer. "Yes?"

The professor finally found his voice. "Go to hell."

Grimes laughed. He couldn't help it. The old man's

obstinacy was refreshing. "As you wish, Professor, as you wish."

With a wave of his hand he summoned Daniels over to him.

"Sir?"

Grimes waved a hand in the professor's direction. "He still has too much fight in him. Soften him up more so we can have another chat. Leave his face alone for now though. I need him to be able to speak."

"Understood."

As Grimes followed Connolly back out of the tent, he could hear the sounds of Daniels's heavy fists thudding into the professor's body like it was a slab of meat.

Two HOURS LATER Grimes stepped back into the tent. He carried a tablet computer in one hand and a cell phone in the other.

The professor was in rough shape. His breath was coming in harsh gasps as he flailed about, trying to stretch far enough to stand on his toes and get a break. Daniels was sitting in a camp chair a few feet away, watching the man struggle and occasionally giving him pointers on how to keep himself from spinning.

Daniels jumped to his feet when he saw Grimes come through the door.

"Take him down," Grimes said.

The other man walked over to the hoist controls and hit the release button. The professor collapsed to the floor.

Grimes picked up the camp chair Daniels had been sitting in and placed it next to the professor. "Sit," he said.

Ephraim only lay there, gasping for breath and shuddering.

At a gesture from Grimes, Daniels hauled the prisoner off the floor and slammed him into the chair. A firm hand on the man's shoulder kept him from sliding off.

"I want you to watch something, Professor. When you're finished I'm going to ask you a question. I would think hard before I answer that question if I were you. Do we understand each other?"

Grimes didn't wait for a reply. He thrust the tablet in front of Ephraim and swiped a finger across the screen. It wasn't a long video, just a few minutes in length, but the screams as his men advanced on one of the female students they'd captured along with the professor was enough to bring tears flooding down the man's cheeks.

Another flick of a finger and the screams were mercifully cut off.

"I want you to take us to the staff, Professor Yellin. I will see to it that the students who agreed to follow you on your escape attempt will come to no further harm. So here's my question, Professor—will you take us to the Staff of Judea?"

30

The transcription work took a couple of hours, after which Annja needed some time to look it over. Ephraim had tried to give her as much information as possible in the short time he'd had available to him and as a result had used abbreviations and drawn connecting arrows between seemingly unrelated notations that took some time to decipher. When she thought she had it all straight in her head, Annja took it to Roux.

"All right," Roux asked as she spread her notes out in front of them. "What have we got?"

"Well, according to Ephraim's notes, the clues in the scroll passages put the staff inside the Fortress Mal'akh near the Makhtesh Gadol."

Roux smiled cheerfully. "Right. Again please, and this time in English, if you don't mind."

That made her laugh, which was something she hadn't done in a while and which she desperately needed. "All right, in English. According the legend, Mal'akh was one of three major fortresses built by

Herod the Great sometime between 30 and 45 BCE
as places of refuge in the event of a revolt by his people. Unlike the other two—Masada and Herodium—
Mal'akh was built in secret, its location known only to
the king's closest family and confidants. Legend states
that Herod slaughtered everyone involved in the con-
struction of the fortress in order to keep its location an
absolute secret. He must have done a decent job, too,
because the fortress has never been found. Most people
think it's a myth."

Roux looked at her closely. "And you? What do you
think?"

"If you'd asked me a month ago I would have said
it's about as real as Noah's Ark. After what I've seen
this week I'd be lining up right behind Noah if you told
me it was going to rain."

She glanced at Roux, saw he had no idea what she
was talking about and quickly continued with, "So,
yes, I do think it is real. More importantly, so does
Ephraim. And he's given us a location where he thinks
we'll find it."

"This Makhtesh Gadol or whatever you call it?"
Roux's French accent butchered the pronunciation.

"Right," she replied, stifling another laugh. She
pulled out a map of Israel that Roux had brought for
their discussion and opened it. She put it down on the
table in front of them so that they had a good look at
the lower half of the country.

"This is the northern Negev," she said, indicating a

section of the map about two-thirds of the way down the length of the country. "And this—" pointing at a small dot on the map labeled Yeruham "—is one of the first of Israel's development towns, new communities created to help settle the influx of refugees from other nations shortly after Israel became a state."

Annja slid her finger across the map to the left, where a long, slim area was shown as a darker shade. "Just to the west is Makhtesh Gadol. A makhtesh," she went on, before Roux could interrupt, "is a peculiar kind of formation caused by massive erosion over a geographically short period of time. Think of it as an oversize box canyon, if that makes sense, formed by the collapse of soft material under the weight of harder material above. It is essentially a deep valley surrounded by steep walls of resistant rock. Gadol means *large* in Hebrew and for many years Makhtesh Gadol was thought to be the largest makhtesh in all of Israel."

"But it's not any longer?" Roux asked.

Annja shook her head. "When it was named, no one knew about Makhtesh Ramon, which is just over forty kilometers in length. In contrast, Makhtesh Gadol is only ten kilometers long and five kilometers wide."

Roux studied the map. "Why would anyone build a fortress at the bottom of a canyon? Your enemies could surround you before you even knew they were coming."

Tactical considerations aside, Annja thought she understood. "Remember, if the legends are correct, Mal'akh was supposed to be the king's ultimate hiding place. He had Masada and Herodium to act as fortresses. Mal'akh was supposed to be his hidden bunker that he could retreat to in the worst-case event. You would want a place like that to have the lowest profile possible and hiding it in a canyon that most people avoid is about as low a profile as you can get."

"And this is where we'll find the staff?"

"According to Ephraim it is and he's rarely been wrong when I've worked with him in the past. It was his reasoning that helped us find the first two caches of treasure listed on the Copper Scroll."

Roux shrugged and Annja took that as tacit approval. "From what I overheard," she continued, "Connolly's goal was the staff all along. Our work at the first two treasure sites was simply a test to see if Ephraim and I were reading the information contained in the scrolls properly. My guess is they'll bypass the rest of the sites and head directly for Mal'akh."

Roux glanced pointedly at the damaged iPad. "Do you have any idea if that was backed up?"

Annja shrugged. "Connolly was paranoid about translations of the scrolls getting out into other people's hands so the only copy in camp was in that. That doesn't mean he doesn't have one somewhere else, though."

"Let's say he does have one," said Roux. "How long will it take him to work this out?" He waved his hands over the notes that Ephraim had given them.

It was a good question. "I don't know. I'm hoping the theft of the iPad sets him back some. If our plan worked and Ephraim managed to make it back to Jerusalem and go to ground, that should slow him up even more. The trouble is that I don't know how much information Connolly had before he started this endeavor. He might have been sitting on the location the entire time."

"Then we need to beat him to it," Roux replied.

Annja borrowed a satellite phone from Roux and tried to call Ephraim, but the professor didn't answer either his cell phone or his office line. A check of her own voice mail told her that he hadn't tried to call, either. That worried her, but there wasn't much she could do about it now.

With time at a premium, Roux made the decision to leave the camp intact and travel immediately to Makhtesh Gadol. Annja agreed, even though she wasn't looking forward to the hours in an SUV driving through the desert.

Annja helped Roux and Henshaw pack what little gear they couldn't leave behind. She, of course, was traveling light, with only the iPad and its case. She thought about leaving them behind, but at the last second had stuffed the damaged unit back into its case and slipped the case into one of Roux's bags. When there was time, she intended to see what other information might be stored on the device. If she could access any of it.

When she went to load the gear, there wasn't a vehicle in sight.

Her confusion must have shown on her face because

Roux laughed. "You didn't think I drove here from Jerusalem, did you?"

"Of course not," she said. "I thought Henshaw drove you."

The comment elicited a rare burst of laughter from Henshaw, who received a scowl from Roux in return. The butler pretended not to notice.

"This way, Ms. Creed," Henshaw said as he hefted a duffel over one shoulder and led the way out of camp along a narrow footpath into the scrubland. They made their way through a thick boulder field for several minutes and then up and over a few hills before coming to a small valley.

Below them sat an unmarked black helicopter.

"Your ride, Ms. Creed."

31

Flying time from their current location to Makhtesh Gadol was a little more than three hours. Annja spent the time going over Ephraim's notes in more detail, doing her best to understand the directions he'd given her. She was so engrossed in her study that she didn't notice they'd arrived until the helicopter began descending.

She looked out the window and took in the canyon below them. It looked like a giant hand had reached down and scooped out a long furrow in the earth. Annja marveled at its beauty. The strata in the rock were clearly visible, the darker bands of harder rock at the top sinking down into the softer, lighter bands at the bottom.

"Can you do a flyby of each canyon wall?" she asked Henshaw over the headset. The canyon was just over five kilometers wide; there shouldn't be an issue.

Henshaw arced the bird over and took them down into the canyon. He got as close as possible to the western wall and then advanced down the length of the canyon, giving both Roux and Annja time to study the stone, looking for any discernible clue as to the location of the fortress. When they were done with the west side, they turned around and did the same in the opposite direction. Truth be told, Annja really didn't expect to find anything. If it was that easy to spot, someone would have done it long before now. She believed in being thorough, however, and not taking the time to do a visual search just seemed wrong.

When the flyby didn't turn up any clues, Annja instructed Henshaw to put the chopper down on the canyon floor close to the south end. Given the width of the canyon he had no problem and quickly had the bird on the ground. They waited for the dust to settle and the rotors to stop spinning before climbing out.

The canyon around them was quiet. Annja felt uneasy all of a sudden. She had the sense she was being watched, being observed. As if the rocks were waiting to see what they would do next.

Then Roux spoke and the feeling vanished.

"Let's gear up and find this staff. We don't know how much time we have before Connolly catches up."

Henshaw pulled several large equipment bags out of the back of the helicopter and lined them up on the ground. Roux and Annja dug through them, taking out the gear they thought they would need and repacking it into smaller daypacks they could carry with them. Annja took water, climbing rope, a set of caming devices, a knife with a decent-size blade, a change of clothes, a compass, a small camp cloth and a headlamp. The usual assortment of gear for a trip into a place where she didn't know what to expect.

When they were finished, Roux turned to Henshaw. "There's no telling what Connolly will do when he gets here. Take the bird up on the ridgeline so you've got more room to run if you need to. Keep us informed by radio as long as you can and defend yourself if need be."

Henshaw nodded. "Of course, sir. Will that be all?"

Annja shook her head, chuckling to herself. Henshaw had to be the most unflappable butler she'd ever met.

Go park the helicopter somewhere else and, oh, by the way, if somebody starts firing at you for no reason, feel free to blow them out of the sky.

Of course, sir. Very good sir.

She and Roux moved a short distance away. Henshaw got back into the helicopter and fired it up. The dust that was whipped up by the spinning rotors caused Annja to turn away for a moment, and when she looked back, Henshaw had taken the chopper out of the canyon to await their return from a safer location.

"Shall we?" Roux asked when the wind and noise had died down.

Annja turned and looked out at the expanse of canyon before them. The canyon itself was a few kilometers in length, its walls climbing hundreds of feet off the ground. The canyon floor, especially near the outer edge, was littered with boulders and the remains of thousands of years worth of rockfalls. The sun beat down, hot and heavy, while a thin breeze barely stirred the air.

Somewhere in there was the entrance to a hidden fortress that no human being had set foot inside in two thousand years. A fortress that they were supposed to find using clues left behind in a couple of ancient scrolls. With nothing but a few pages of notes and some old-fashioned guesswork.

Piece of cake.

"Let's go!"

"WELL?"

Douglas made one last adjustment to the tracking device on the table, then closed the access panel and handed it to Grimes.

"Finished, sir. Sorry it took so long."

"Just as long as it works, Douglas."

"Oh, it will, sir. I guarantee it."

Connolly will hold you to that, son. Grimes kept that thought to himself. By now the men who worked for him knew better than to boast about something without being able to back it up. All Grimes had to do was flip this switch on the side and they'd know, one way or another, whether Douglas had done his job properly.

Connolly was concerned about the Creed woman, which meant that Grimes had to be, as well. What bothered the boss the most was the way in which Creed had been rescued by those horsemen last night just as

Grimes had effectively run her to ground. The speed at which they had appeared and the way they had intentionally blocked the security teams' fire to protect her suggested she'd been working with the intruders all along.

Creed had escaped and had taken the iPad containing a good portion of their information about the staff with her. Connolly wanted her tracked down and dealt with as swiftly as possible. The project Grimes had assigned to Douglas was intended to do just that.

He handed the tracker to Connolly. "Thought I'd let you do the honors."

Connolly turned the device over a few times in his hands. "So how does this work again?"

What difference does it make? Grimes wanted to say. It will work and that's all that matters. But Connolly was the boss and Grimes had survived this long by doing what the boss wanted.

"There's a GPS transmitter in your tablet, just like the GPS transmitters in a cell phone. Douglas hacked into the cell network to get your individual GPS signal and then modified the tracking software in the handheld so that it would look for your tablet rather than the beacon it had originally been designed to hunt down. He also extended the reach of the device by allowing it to use our satellite network. When you flick the switch, the tracker should show us the current GPS position of your iPad. All we have to do from there is follow it."

Connolly looked up and met his gaze. "And where we find my tablet, you expect to find Annja."

"I do."

"Then what are we waiting for?"

As Grimes looked on, Connolly flicked the switch.

For a moment, nothing happened. The screen stayed blank. Connolly opened his mouth to say something but Grimes held up a hand. "It's just calibrating. Give it a moment."

As soon as the words left his mouth the tracker beeped once and a red dot appeared at the bottom right of the screen. Next to that dot were coordinates: N30°55′30″, E34°58′52″.

"Douglas?"

The former commando took note of the numbers and then punched them into his computer. A moment later a name popped up on the screen.

Makhtesh Gadol.

32

If Roux hadn't been watching the hawk, they wouldn't have found the cave entrance as quickly as they did.

After Henshaw had taken off, they stuck close to the east wall of the canyon, following it for about a kilometer to where a series of caves became visible in the walls above them. Annja guessed there had to be at least two hundred of them, if not more. They were as common as a warren of rabbits left to breed indiscriminately for years.

According to Ephraim's notes, the entrance to the fortress was hidden in one of those caves. To find the right one, they were to look for the symbol of the "guide in the night," a reference, Ephraim believed, to the ancient Jewish belief that God led Moses and the Israelites across the desert during their years of exile with a pillar of cloud by day and a pillar of fire by night.

But what did a stone pillar of fire look like, really? There had to be just as many strange rock formations in the area as there were caves. Would they even know it when they saw it? And would it not have eroded after all this time?

Only one way to find out.

They began the slow, painstaking search. They started with the larger cave mouths closest to the ground, checking each one for the expected symbol before using some of the chalk Annja had brought along to mark off those that had been investigated from the dozens of others around them. With so little information to go on, they were careful to explore as many possible candidates as they could, a decision that was going to add to the time it would take to complete the task but would also keep them from overlooking the right cave because they didn't exactly know what they were looking for.

They'd been at it for only a half hour when the hawk caught Roux's attention. He watched it circling high above them for a few minutes while Annja checked out the next hole in the canyon wall. At first he'd taken it for some kind of drone, it circled so perfectly above their position. He'd drawn a handgun out of his pack and gotten ready to try to shoot it down, when the bird folded back its wings and went into a steep dive.

Roux followed it down as it plunged toward the earth, no doubt about to make some other desert creature's life a good degree shorter, and he watched as it disappeared behind a vertical pillar of rock that seemed to twist and move in the bright light of the afternoon sun.

The pillar of fire!

The hawk burst from cover, a mouse in its talons, and Roux saluted it as it flew away. He kept his gaze on the pillar from behind which the hawk had emerged and called out to Annja.

"I think I've found it."

She was just emerging from a cave several yards to his left and quickly joined him. He pointed out the formation to her and the two of them made their way over.

Up close, the optical illusion that made the stone pillar look like it was flickering back and forth like the flames of a fire disappeared, leaving them staring at nothing more than a tall hunk of freestanding rock. Behind it, half-hidden in the shadow cast by the ten-foot column, was a narrow opening in the rock.

As cave mouths went it wasn't much. Just a small opening near the floor of the canyon, so low that Annja had to get down on her knees and bend to look inside. The sunlight barely reached inside the hole, so Annja dug her headlamp out of her pack and put it on. With the help of its light she could see that the cave opened up considerably once you got past the first several feet. A bend in the tunnel kept her from seeing too far inside, but it seemed clear that beyond the cave mouth was a rather substantial tunnel leading deeper under the cliff wall.

Annja felt a stab of excitement.

"I'm going to check it out," she told Roux. Before her companion could reply she had stripped off her pack and, pushing it ahead of her, climbed inside the cave mouth flat on her stomach.

There wasn't a lot of wiggle room. The sides of the tunnel were very close; she barely had enough space to wiggle her hips back and forth to get some momentum going as she pulled herself forward with her hands. For just a second she thought about the several million tons of rock hanging suspended just above her head, waiting to come crashing down and bury her for all eternity. Then she banished the thought. If it was going to come down there wasn't anything she could do about it, anyway.

After several minutes of effort she slid out of the entrance tunnel and into a small chamber. By the light of her headlamp she could see that it was roughly circular, with another tunnel mouth opening directly across from the one she'd just entered through. This other opening was much larger, however. Neither she nor Roux would have any difficulty walking upright.

Her light fell on the space directly above the tunnel mouth and she froze, her eyes widening at the sight. Carved into the lintel of the tunnel mouth was an intricately stylized pillar of flames and several words written in what could only be Hebrew. She couldn't read them, but that was okay. She already knew what they said.

Welcome, Annja.

Or, at least, that's what they said to her.

"Anything?" Roux called from outside.

Oh, nothing much, just the hidden entrance to King Herod's long-lost refuge.

She saved Roux the sarcasm. "Yes, this is it!" she called back. "Watch yourself. It's a tight squeeze."

A few minutes and a lot of grumbling and cursing later, Roux stood by her side. He glanced around, saw the writing above the tunnel mouth and studied it for a moment. "With a pillar of fire, He led them to the Promised Land."

Annja looked at him, surprised. "I didn't know you could read Hebrew."

"You never asked," Roux replied smugly, before heading deeper into the mountain.

They traveled forward for another fifteen minutes without finding anything of interest. The tunnel meandered through several twists and turns, so much so that it became obvious the workmen had relied on an existing passage through the rock rather than carving their own straighter course. Aside from the carving at the entrance, the only clues that this was a manmade passage were the sconces set into the walls every twenty-five feet.

At last they emerged into an open chamber that was a good fifty feet across and at least two stories high. A wide beam of sunlight blazed down from the ceiling, the result of a perfectly placed shaft bored through to the surface that would capture the light at a specific time each day, Annja surmised. She turned to follow the sunbeam and gasped when she saw what it revealed.

Just as with the ruins at Petra in Jordan, the entire rock wall at the far end of the chamber had been sculpted so it looked like the front of a temple building, complete with obviously false windows and balconies on the second floor and three very real doorways directly ahead on the first. Two large statues of a man Annja took to be King Herod stood on either side of the trio of doors, staring across the chamber at them with stern expressions. In a subtle hint of what lay inside, each statue held a shepherd's crook in their hands.

Annja and Roux grinned at each other, their thoughts on the prize before them.

33

They spotted the other chopper from the air and made a couple of passes over the site to be on the safe side. Even from a distance Grimes recognized the make and model. The Bell 427 was a fairly common utility bird. The twin engines and four-blade rotor system gave it both speed and versatility in the air, never mind a range of over seven hundred kilometers. This one was painted black and was completely bare of any kind of insignia or marking, including tail numbers. It looked abandoned, so Grimes ordered his man to set their own bird down a few dozen yards away. As soon as they were on the ground, Grimes, Beck and Daniels were advancing on the other helicopter, weapons in hand.

With the other two men covering him, Grimes threw open the door and discovered that his initial impression had been right—the cockpit was empty. Dust hadn't had time to build up on the windshield and the frame, however.

Grimes had little doubt the chopper belonged to

Annja and whoever she had managed to enlist to help her. His opinion was confirmed when an order for Daniels and Beck to search the vehicle turned up Connolly's iPad, complete with its leather case. The bullet hole through the center of it was unfortunate. Grimes knew Mitchell was not going to be happy about that.

The hair on the back of his neck stood on end as he suddenly felt like he was being watched. He spun around, his weapon up, and surveyed the boulder field surrounding their landing area, looking for a telltale hint of movement or the flash of sunlight on the glass of a spotting scope or pair of binoculars. Nothing.

Still, the feeling persisted.

He turned to face his own chopper and held up two fingers, then pointed to the area around them. Two more of his men—he couldn't be certain who it was at this distance and frankly he didn't care as long as the job got done—climbed down from the chopper and headed in the direction he'd pointed, searching for whoever might be out there.

Better safe than sorry, he thought.

Grimes waited impatiently until the men—Gardner and Johnson, as it turned out—returned fifteen minutes later.

"Anything?" he asked.

It was Gardner who answered him. "Looks like two people exited the aircraft, and then wandered up here before descending into the canyon. I'm guessing a man and a woman, as one set of tracks is deeper than the other. Might even be a third individual, but I'm less certain of that. Could just be a weak sign from one of the first two."

"All right. Keep your eyes open. Something doesn't feel right."

Grimes had long ago learned to trust his instincts and right now those instincts were telling him they weren't alone. Still, Gardner had said there might be one unconfirmed individual, not fifty. How much damage could one guy do?

If there was somebody out there, they'd neutralize him when the time came.

Grimes returned to the chopper and brought Connolly up to speed. As expected, the boss wasn't happy about the tablet, but when Grimes let him know that they seemed to be close on the heels of Annja and whoever was assisting her, Connolly forgot about it in favor of focusing on the real issue—beating Creed to the staff.

"What are we doing screwing around up here for, anyway?" he asked Grimes, the irritation plain on his face. "Creed's down there somewhere." He pointed at the lip of the canyon. "That's where we should be, as well. Get in and let's get down there where we belong. We're not going to find the staff up here."

The canyon was wide enough that they could take off and land in the middle of it, saving them the effort of a descent, but Grimes was leery about doing so.

"It's my guess that Annja arrived here ahead of us and is no doubt hunting for the entrance to the fortress even as we speak. We only made one pass over the canyon. When we came back to take a look at the chopper, we did so at an oblique angle and that should have dampened the sound considerably. I doubt anyone knows we're here."

He glanced over, saw Connolly was getting impatient and wrapped it up. "Right now we have a tactical advantage that we'd be foolish to waste, and landing in the center of the canyon would do just that."

"Fine," Connolly replied, his irritation quickly growing to anger. "Find us a way down and let's stop wasting time."

Grimes looked at the professor. "I'm sure our guest would be happy to help with that, right, Professor? And before you answer, let me remind you that the continued health and welfare of your students depends on how useful you are to us."

The archaeologist stared at him for a moment. "There's a trail to the canyon floor from the south escarpment. Once we're at the bottom we need to look for the rock formation mentioned in the scroll."

Grimes smiled. "Well done, Professor, well done."

While the men gathered the gear they were going to need for what lay ahead, Grimes instructed the pilot to take the helicopter a safe distance away and to wait for Grimes's radio call for extraction. Just because his men hadn't found anyone watching them from the surrounding scrub didn't mean there wasn't someone out there. Grimes had no intention of leaving their transport home out here like a sitting duck.

Yellin led them to a narrow defile that bisected the south end of the canyon, revealing a trail that led downward. Hamilton and Beck took point, their weapons at the ready. After them came Professor Yellin, Grimes and then Connolly. Bringing up the rear were Daniels, Johnson, Douglas and Gardner.

The trail was narrow and steep, with plenty of loose stone underfoot to trip the unwary. Because of the condition of the trail, it took Grimes a while to notice it was man-made. Every now and then he could see where ancient steps had been cut into the rockface in particularly difficult sections to help ease downward passage. The work was cleverly done. He wouldn't have noticed it if he hadn't known the fortress was nearby and been looking for some evidence of that.

Once they reached the canyon floor, Grimes gave the group five minutes to rest and grab some water before they set out again. According to the professor, they were looking for a rock formation that looked like a pillar of fire. Once they found that, they would use it to locate the cave mouth that marked the entrance to the fortress.

It sounded like a load of rubbish. Ten years ago he would have laughed outright at the idea of hunting for a column of stone carved to look like a giant flame, but time and experience had changed his viewpoint. He'd accompanied Connolly on enough of these crazy expeditions to know not to judge "crazy" by face value.

It was that understanding that started him thinking about himself, rather than his employer, for a change as they made their way across the dusty canyon floor. He'd supported Connolly for years because the man's agendas often coincided with Grimes's own. There was a lot to be said for accomplishing your own goals by using someone else's money. But if even half of what was said about the power of the staff was true, it would be foolhardy to allow it to fall into someone else's hands. Far better to use it for his own ends.

It would be easy. The men were loyal to him rather than Connolly. He'd handpicked each and every one of them. If he gave the order, they'd turn on Connolly in a heartbeat. Professor Yellin was cooperating only because he was being forced to. That wouldn't change if Grimes seized control. Out here in the desert, there was no way for Connolly to get help, either. It would all be a fait accompli by the time they got back to civilization.

The more Grimes thought about it, the more he liked the idea. He decided to bide his time, wait for the right moment and then make his move.

Locating the stone formation they were searching for, the one that looked like a pillar of fire, took them almost three hours. During their first search of the cliff face they went right past it without noticing. It was only when the professor decided they'd gone too far and turned them around for a pass in the opposite direction that they saw it. The late-afternoon sun set the rocks around them blazing and even Grimes had to admit the column did look like an oversize flame.

The cave didn't look like much—a child-size hole at the base of the cliff wall—but the recent boot prints in the loose earth just outside it told them beyond a doubt they were on the right track. Grimes held the others back while Gardner had a look and confirmed his earlier reading—two people, most likely a male and a female traveling together.

Even better, Gardner thought that the tracks were less than an hour old.

"Hamilton! Crawl in there and check it out."

"Yes, sir."

Hamilton wiggled his way into the narrow passageway. It was a tight fit, given his broad shoulders, but he managed to push himself along with several hard thrusts of his legs. A few minutes after he'd climbed inside there was a sharp hiss as he lit a magnesium flare, the light spilling back down the tunnel to the rest of them. Another moment passed and then they heard his voice echo back along the tunnel.

"All clear, sir."

Grimes turned to the others. "Johnson and Daniels, you're on watch. I want you to guard this entrance and make sure no one goes in or out without us. Douglas, Gardner, Beck, you've got rear guard. Follow us in."

Ready or not, Annja, here we come.

34

"Right, left or center?" Roux asked, indicating the three entrances outlined in the light ahead of them.

Annja opened her mouth to reply, then paused. She didn't know. She didn't remember Ephraim's notes mentioning anything about choosing a door. Just to be safe, she set her pack down and dug the pages containing Ephraim's scribbled notes out of the front pocket so she could double check.

Nope. Nothing there.

"We're going to have to guess," she said in resignation.

"Okay, I vote for the center."

"The center? Why the center?"

"Why not?"

Annja frowned. "Don't you think we need a more logical reason to make that choice than 'just because'?"

Roux laughed. "No. And have I ever told you that you overthink things?"

Three doors. Which one to choose?

Like Roux with the middle entry, she would have taken the right one without much thought; it was a natural reaction for right-handed people. That there was the problem. Annja knew from experience that the guys who designed places like this were cut from the same cloth. Not only were they paranoid—knowing you could be beheaded at the king's whim for the slightest infraction—but they were also devious.

She tried to put herself into the architect's shoes. She didn't know much about the history of Mal'akh, but as a last fortress and refuge for King Herod, it made sense that the architect would make it difficult for an enemy to reach him. If it had been up to her, she would have booby-trapped two of the three entrances, at the least.

So if the natural inclination for most people is to take the right passage, wouldn't that be the one the architect would most likely use as a false entry?

On the other hand, as a Jew, Herod would have seen the left hand as the unclean one and therefore might have objected to using that passage as the entrance into his private sanctum.

Which brought her right back to Roux's suggestion, the center passage.

I'm probably going to regret this.

"Fine," she said. "Center, it is."

They approached the opening cautiously and shone their lights over the threshold. A narrow corridor continued beyond as far as they could see. Unlike the previous corridor, this one was squared off, like a corridor in a freestanding building rather than the rounded natural tunnel they'd just left behind.

A light breeze was blowing down the hall, just enough to stir the dust on the ground slightly, and Annja found herself marveling at the engineering involved to funnel fresh air this deep beneath the surface. It made her question what other wonders they were going to find in the halls ahead.

Not seeing anything to concern her, Annja stepped over the threshold.

There was a sharp click.

She froze, not daring to move, thoughts of pressure plates and booby traps racing through her mind.

The click had come from behind her.

Without moving her feet or lower body, Annja turned her head and looked back.

Roux was standing there, pistol in hand. He slapped the magazine back into place again with a sharp click.

He realized she was watching him. "What?" he said. "Better safe than sorry, right?"

Her heart pounding in her chest, Annja wanted to strangle him but she settled for a mumbled "right" and turned back to what she'd been doing.

They followed the corridor beyond for a short distance before coming to another doorway. This one was shorter than the one before, and they had to duck to pass through it. On the other side was a small room.

The chamber was roughly ten by twelve, if Annja had to hazard a guess, but it seemed smaller because much of the floor space was gobbled up by a large ceremonial-looking pool. The water in it was clear and appeared to be reasonably deep; Annja guessed it was at least six feet, if not deeper. The pool was surrounded by a low stone wall that didn't quite reach her knees but was just high enough to contain the water.

As Roux walked over to look inside the pool, Annja headed for the far wall, searching for a way out. At first glance there didn't seem to be one and that didn't make much sense.

Plop!

Annja spun around. Roux had a rock in his hand and was getting ready to drop it into the water.

"What are you doing?" she asked.

"I was curious how deep the water was. It seemed rather deceiving so…"

That was as far as Roux got. A loud grinding sound filled the chamber and both he and Annja spun around to the door.

A thick stone slab was already more than halfway across the entrance.

"No, no, no, no!" Annja cried as she ran across the chamber, frantically looking for something to jam into the opening to keep the slab from closing all the way.

With a muffled thud the slab fell into place.

Annja reached it about the same time Roux did and they both threw their shoulders against it, trying to lever it back open.

It was no use. The stone was too heavy. They couldn't even budge it.

Roux cursed.

Annja turned back to find another way out when the surface of the water caught her eye. A moment ago it had been clear. Now there was a spot of color.

Specifically, red.

"What on earth?"

She hurried over to take a look.

A thin spiral of red was filling the center of the pool, lazily rising up from somewhere at the bottom. Already she was having trouble seeing the bottom as the red began to drift throughout the pool.

The thick, viscous nature of the stuff reminded her of blood.

Even as she watched, the water in the pool, now tainted with a slight blush of red, sloshed over the side of the wall. It wasn't much, just a cupful really. But then that one little breach became two, then three. In the space of a few seconds, water was dripping over the stone containment wall in half a dozen places, pooling on what had seconds before been dry ground.

"Roux, we have to get out of here."

He spoke without turning. "Brilliant deduction, Annja. I salute your powers of reasoning. Of course we have to get out of here. The only question is determining—"

"Roux!"

He turned back to her, the indignation plain on his face. "What? I know we—"

"Look."

He did. He took in the water—now a much deeper red than it had been only seconds before—and the speed at which it was overflowing and that was all it took. He immediately left off trying to force the door and began searching the walls.

Annja started on the other side of the door and began to do the same thing. There has to be a way out. You don't build a room with no way out of it unless…

…unless you wanted to trap someone in it.

She glanced back at the pool.

The water was flowing much faster now, spilling out on all sides and beginning to accumulate.

She ran her hands over the surface of the wall. She was looking for a nook, a niche—anything that might conceal a trigger to stop what was happening around her. She'd encountered hundreds of booby traps during her years as an archaeologist and adventurer, and more often than not there was a safety, something that could be used to stop from springing the trap or reset it.

The question was whether they would find it in time.

Warm water splashed against her lower leg. The pool now covered the floor about an inch deep.

The smell of the stuff hit her. That unmistakable metallic scent that clung to the back of her throat and made her want to retch.

Her first inclination had been right; it *was* blood.

And at the rate it was rising, if they didn't do something soon, they were going to drown in it.

CONNOLLY AND HIS GROUP stood in front of the entrance to the fortress, flares held high, staring at footprints in the dust on the floor that led to the center doorway.

Clearly Annja and her companion had passed this way.

Grimes glanced at the professor and noticed a frown cross the man's face.

Interesting.

"Is there a problem, Professor?" he asked aloud, startling the others as he broke the silence. His words seemed to echo in the large space.

"No," the older man said. He gestured. "We need to use the left entrance."

He took a step toward it but Grimes stopped him with a hand on his elbow.

"Why the left?" Grimes asked.

"The place of honor at the table is always on the right. That's the obvious choice, therefore it won't be safe. It will be, how do you say it, booby-trapped in some way?"

Grimes kept eye contact with the man, looking for a sign that he was lying. The professor didn't even bat an eye.

"All right, we'll take the left passage," Connolly told Grimes. "And the professor will go first."

35

With the pool rising around them at a rapidly increasing rate, Annja knew time was of the essence. She tried to ignore it, tried to pretend that every heartbeat didn't sound like the ticking of some massive clock, but it was no use. That's exactly what it *did* sound like.

Not finding anything in their respective positions, they moved farther along the walls in opposite directions, broadening their search.

As the minutes ticked past, the bloody water rose around them, reaching their ankles, then their knees, then midthigh. It stank to high heaven. As the water rose higher it became harder to think as the air remaining in the room became polluted with the carbon dioxide they were exhaling.

Annja glanced at where Roux was standing, looking up and letting the beam of his headlamp play across the rock surface that was really only a few feet from his head.

"Anything?" she asked, pausing in her own search for a moment.

"Nothing," he replied.

For what seemed like the millionth time, she glanced around, but the room was empty, except for the pool.

The pool.

She turned toward the source of their trouble, only to realize the low walls that marked the edge of the ceremonial basin had long since disappeared beneath the rising liquid. If it hadn't been for the bubbling fount in the center of the space that marked where the fluid was being pushed up from below, she wouldn't even have known it had been there in the first place.

The blood had to be coming from somewhere. The flow hadn't been triggered until Roux had dropped something into the pool, which meant there was some mechanical process attached to either the height of the water or the additional weight on the bottom of the pool. Annja guessed the latter. When the stone hit the bottom, it must have triggered a sluice of some kind that, when opened, flooded the room. Given how quickly the room was filling, that sluice had to be pretty big.

Annja stripped off her pack and handed it to Roux. "I've got an idea. Hold this," she told him. She unzipped the pack and dug out her climbing rope. She tied one end around her waist, knotting it securely and handed the other to Roux.

"We don't have time to waste, Annja. What do you think you are doing?"

"Getting our asses out of here, that's what. All this stuff—" she waved a hand at the crimson tide that was nearly waist-deep at this point "—has to come from somewhere. The pipe that's pushing it in here is probably our only way out. I'm going to dive down and see if it's wide enough for us to fit through. While I do that, you're going to hold on to the rope. If you feel three tugs in a row, I want you to start pulling me back up as fast as you can."

He stared at her. "You're nuts, you know that?"

"Yep, but nuts is better than drowning here, don't you think?"

"Hurry," he said.

She sloshed her way over to the edge of the pool, using the fountainlike bubble in the center to guess where the edge was. She still managed to bang her knee on the retaining wall when she guessed incorrectly.

Once in position she took a couple of deep breaths, flashed a thumbs-up at Roux and then dove over the wall into the ceremonial pool.

Annja had always been a good swimmer, and that helped her now as she cut downward through the thick, viscous liquid. It was warm and seemed to press in at her from all sides, but she did her best not to pay attention to it. If she started thinking about where all that blood came from she'd probably have a break with reality.

There was a strong current coming from somewhere below here, which was exactly what she was looking for. With one hand against the inner wall of the pool and the other stretched out straight ahead to keep her from swimming headfirst into the bottom of the pool, Annja propelled herself downward with a couple of kicks from her powerful legs. She reached the bottom and tread there for a moment, fighting both her own upward buoyancy and the push of the current that was trying to shove her back to the surface. She let the flow of the water tell her where that current was coming from—the side of the pool off to her left rather than the bottom—and then struck out toward it.

By following the inner wall, she was able to come up on the opening from one side without being shoved away by the current. Her heart was beating in her ears and her lungs were starting to protest the lack of fresh oxygen as she reached out toward the flow.

She felt a surge of hope when she realized that the opening was, in fact, quite large. Her hand encountered a wide curve that slid out of reach in either direction. By sticking her hand directly into the flow she discovered that the current wasn't strong. She thought she could swim against it.

That left her with a decision to make.

Turn around, resurface and tell Roux what she had found, or try to swim up the sluice to see if it provided a way out. If she chose the latter and there was no fresh air within just a short distance on the other side, she was in trouble. She'd black out long before she made it back out again, current or no current, and that would be that.

If she didn't take the chance, however, they might head up the sluice only to find it narrowed considerably just a few feet beyond the opening and they'd die, anyway.

Better to know for sure.

Even the few seconds she'd taken making up her mind might make the difference between life and death so Annja didn't hesitate any longer. She kicked off and swam directly into the current, like a fish swimming upstream, fighting against the push of the water as hard as she could.

The water slammed her into the side of the channel and tried to force her back out, but she kicked and clawed her way forward, her lungs screaming now. She clenched her jaw shut and pushed on, determined to get to the end.

The angle of the channel changed. She was no longer swimming horizontally but was now moving diagonally upward. She kicked harder, pulling at the bloody water around her with everything she had.

Like a whale breaching the surface of the ocean, Annja burst out of the channel. She couldn't see—the water was way too thick—but she could sense space around her opening up.

She gulped down a great lungful of air. She could feel the warm, thick water flowing down her head and across her face. The smell made her want to gag. She tried to wipe it away with hands as equally slick.

Her headlamp, still strapped tightly around her forehead, showed she was in a room similar to the one she had just left behind. They would have been identical, except this one had a closed stone doorway on the right side of the room rather than the left.

That's when she understood. When the trap was sprung, the liquid that had previously filled this room was sucked into the sluice and deposited in the room she'd just left.

Roux!

Annja sucked in a deep breath and dove back under, reversing her previous route. This time it was much easier. The current snatched her the moment she entered it and she shot through the channel like a bullet from a gun, to come bursting out the other end.

She surfaced…and promptly banged her head on the ceiling.

"Oh, good. I was starting to think I was going to drown all on my own. Nice of you to join me in this once-in-a-lifetime opportunity."

Annja turned around and found Roux treading water nearby, their respective backpacks slung one over each arm. The water was just below his neck. He smiled at her, steadfastly refusing to show anything but bravery right to the very end. A knight of old.

"Nobody's drowning today," Annja said. "There's a way out." She filled him in on what she had learned.

Roux's smile turned genuine as he passed her pack over to her. "If we wait until the last moment, the pressure will have slackened considerably and we should be able to traverse the connecting tunnel without fighting against the current."

He was right. If they could steel their nerves as the water rose higher, by the time they ducked beneath the surface and reached the tunnel, the flow might even have stopped altogether.

They agreed to wait it out. When the time came Annja would go first, the rope still tied about her waist. Roux would wait a moment, letting a few feet of rope play out between them, and then he would follow behind her. Since Annja had already traversed the route twice, it would be up to her to locate the tunnel mouth and guide them in.

Rather than take the chance that their packs would get caught on something en route, they agreed to tie them to the end of the rope and let them sink. When they made it out the other side, they could haul them along in their wake.

By the time they had the plan all figured out and the packs tied off on the end of the rope, the bloody water had risen to just below their noses.

"See you on the other side," she said, then ducked below the surface before Roux had a chance to respond.

36

Thank heavens for waterproof packs. Annja stripped off her soaked clothes and dropped them in a sodden pile on the floor. Somewhere behind her, she heard Roux doing the same.

They'd managed to make it through the tunnel before running out of air or fluid to swim through. The latter was something she hadn't even thought about until she'd burst through the tunnel into the room on the other end and watched the last of the water disappearing into the opening she'd emerged from. She realized that Roux was about to be left hanging in midair when the water around him disappeared and so she scrambled out of the hold and started pulling on the rope to drag him higher as the seconds ticked past. In the end she'd been left to brace herself against the other edge while he pulled himself hand over hand up the rope.

They'd looked like something out of a horror movie gone wrong.

She'd started stripping off her clothes immediately

and it had taken ten seconds for Roux to follow suit. Ever the gentlemen, he'd turned his back.

She drew the combat knife she'd brought along and used the spine of the blade like a squeegee, sluicing her body as best she could. She used a little of the water she'd brought along to clean her face and hands with the camp cloth.

She couldn't exactly say she was clean when she was finished, but she certainly felt better. She dried herself with the cloth and then pulled on her change of clothes. She grimaced at the squishing sound her foot made as she slipped it back into her saturated boot, but without another pair of shoes she had no choice.

"Are you decent?" Roux asked.

When she assured him that she was, they turned to face each other. Annja took one look and started laughing. Roux looked ridiculous, with his white hair and beard red in the spots he'd missed and pink in those where he'd gotten most of the liquid off. He still had splotches on his skin, the tip of one ear and on his left arm. Annja knew she must look equally ridiculous.

"Perhaps I'll let you choose which passage to take next time," Roux said, which only set them both off a second time.

Annja had just straightened up when she saw a frog hop across the stone floor a few feet behind Roux.

It was a small frog, no more than two inches long, a brilliant yellow that stuck out against the red-stained stones.

Annja couldn't believe what she was seeing and for a moment couldn't say a word. She could only stare at the frog as it hopped closer.

And closer still.

"Where the heck did they come from?" Roux said, pointing.

Afraid to look but more afraid not to, Annja followed his pointing finger. Her light flashed across a wave of yellow frogs, just like the first, that were advancing toward them from somewhere near the edge of the room. She brought her head up, letting the light play across the rear wall.

It was studded with hundreds of little holes, warrens really, and emerging from them were more of the yellow frogs.

Roux leaned toward the nearest of them, and Annja nearly had a heart attack.

"Don't touch them!" she yelled, more sharply than she intended.

Roux straightened immediately. He saw the expression on her face and said, "You don't think…?"

"I do. If those aren't golden dart frogs, I'm a rhesus monkey."

Roux took a healthy step away from the frog and closer to her. "That's not possible," he said, though his actions suggested differently. "The dart frog is native to South America. It is way too hot and dry for them to survive here."

One of the frogs jumped too close for comfort. There

was a silvery flash and the frog was split in two. Annja pulled her arm back, but didn't put away the sword.

"I don't have a clue how it's possible, but I know a dart frog when I see one." She didn't say what they both knew; the *Phyllobates terribilis,* or golden dart frog, excreted a deadly toxin through its skin. It made puffer fish toxin look like a mild irritant. One touch and it was all over.

More of the little creatures hopped closer and Annja's sword flashed again. And again.

She was drawing back for a short stab to take out a fourth when the connections suddenly flared in her mind.

Water into blood.

A wave of poisonous frogs.

The staff of Aaron.

"The ten plagues of Egypt."

"What?" Roux used the toe of his boot to flip a frog halfway across the room. It did little good; a moment later another hopped forward.

Annja's head snapped up as she refocused on what was happening around her and her arm thrust and slashed and jabbed, opening up space around them to buy a few moments.

"According to the Bible, ten plagues were called down upon Egypt when the Pharaoh refused to let the Israelites leave. The first two involved all the rivers in Egypt turning to blood and the second was a plague of poisonous frogs that infested the countryside."

Annja scooped up her pack, shook it to dislodge the frog that had decided it made a good rest stop and slung it over her shoulder. "We need to get out of here, Roux, and we need to do it before things get worse."

"For once we're in one hundred percent agreement."

Together they began to make their way across the room, toward the door they could see on the far wall. Like in the room they'd left behind, this door was closed, but Annja was desperately hoping that they could find a way to open it even though they'd had no luck with the other.

The universe wouldn't frown on them like that twice in one day, now would it?

As they made their way across the room, the frogs seemed drawn to them. As if attracted by their heat or their smell. Annja was doing the best she could to poke and slash the frogs back.

Roux reached the door first and began hunting for a way to open it. He ran his hands over the stone, searching.

While he was doing that, Annja was holding off the frogs—none had gotten through yet, a real testament to her skill with her blade—but it was only a matter of time before the frogs overwhelmed them. A glance at the back wall showed more and more of the yellow snouts emerging from the recesses there.

"A little faster, Roux."

"I'm trying, Annja, I'm trying."

"Well, try harder!"

He muttered something underneath his breath in French that she missed.

Probably a good thing.

There were hundreds of the little yellow terrors by now, with more emerging every minute. They were jumping all over one another and the floor looked like it had become nothing more than a seething mass of living tissue slowly hopping in her direction.

Annja was using the tip of her sword to stab those that drew too close and the flat of the blade to swat the ones that tried to jump at them. Her sword flashed over and over again, the blade now thick with blood and guts.

Concerned she wouldn't be able to get them all, she drew her commando knife and began going at them with two blades instead of one. She wanted to scream, but clamped her mouth shut.

Suddenly Roux cried, "Got it!" and a loud grinding noise filled the room as the door slid slowly to the right, revealing another chamber beyond. Roux reached back and dragged Annja through the doorway after him, trying to put as much distance as possible between them and the frogs.

As they stumbled forward, they belatedly realized that they had emerged not only into a well-lit chamber but one that was a far cry from empty.

Guns swiveled in their direction and the familiar voice of Grimes said, "Well, well, well. What have we here?"

37

Grimes just couldn't believe his luck.

After entering the fortress proper through the doorway chosen by Professor Yellin, they'd spent the past twenty minutes wandering through a series of passages that seemed to double and triple back on one another without really leading anywhere. The professor had assured him they were on the right track, but Grimes had been having second thoughts about the wisdom of trusting the man and had ordered the group take a five-minute break while he sorted it out in his head. He'd been sitting there, going over his options, when a section of the wall had ground open and Annja and a strange man stumbled out. No sooner had they cleared the threshold than the door slid shut again, sealing them on this side of the barrier and whatever was clearly chasing them on the other.

"If it isn't the great archaeologist herself, Annja Creed." Grimes studied her in mock deference. "And, look, she brought a friend. Is that… Could it be… Yes, I think it is…Roux."

"Kill them," Connolly said.

"You'll never find the staff if you kill her." The professor was on his feet, standing in front of the other two prisoners. He had a determined look on his face, which caused Grimes to laugh.

"Look around you, Professor." Grimes extended his arms for emphasis. "We've found the fortress. We don't need you to guide us anymore."

"Is that what you think? My Lord, but you're a fool. Why don't you ask Annja what happens when you choose the wrong door around here?"

Grimes noticed the blood splattered on Annja for the first time.

"If you expect my continued cooperation," Ephraim went on, "you will bring Ms. Creed and her companion with us."

Grimes opened his mouth to argue and was surprised when Connolly cut him off.

"Do as he says, Grimes. We're wasting time."

"Yes, sir."

There was no sense arguing. He could always kill them later if they got in his way. Connolly, too, for that matter.

He'd seen Annja pull a sword out of thin air twice now and he had no intention of allowing it to happen a third time.

"Beck, tie Annja's hands behind her back. Make sure

the rope's good and tight. Douglas, search them and their bags. Take anything useful, leave the rest behind."

Grimes got the rest of their group on their feet. Fresh flares were activated and they set out once more. Annja and Roux were put in the middle of the marching order just behind the professor. Grimes gave Gardner a break from point and moved Daniels up to that position instead, wanting the man at the front to be fresh and on the lookout for these traps the professor had warned of.

They passed through several empty chambers and Grimes was starting to think the professor was wasting his time when they walked through another doorway and emerged into a massive cavern. The roof soared somewhere high above, well out of sight, while in front of them gaped an enormous chasm that bisected their route of travel. A thin finger of stone reached out across the gap to the other side of the cavern where the passage they'd been following continued onward in the same direction. The ceiling soared upward, as well, disappearing into the darkness high above their heads.

Grimes frowned. He didn't like the look of this place. The bridge had clearly been designed to intimidate and he had to admit it was having the desired effect. The path was worn smooth with the passage of countless feet, indicating that it was safe to cross. That by no means removed his anxiety. There were no railings— nothing to hold on to. Nothing to use to keep from falling if one's feet slipped out from under in the middle of the crossing.

And if they fell…

Grimes leaned over the edge and dropped the flare he held. He watched it fall for what seemed like forever. In the end, it traveled so far that it winked out of sight. He had a very strong suspicion that it still hadn't hit bottom at that point.

If they fell, they were dead. It was as simple as that.

Grimes stepped back from the edge and walked over to the professor. He pointed across the bridge. "You're positive that's the way we have to go?"

"Yes."

Grimes studied the man's face carefully, looking for some trace of deception. It seemed the man was telling the truth.

"All right," Grimes announced to the group. "We're going across that bridge. Single file, three feet between each individual. If you slip, you're on your own. I won't have one clumsy idiot taking the rest of the party with them."

"You need to untie Annja," Roux spoke up. "She's going to need her hands free for balance or she's never going to make it across."

Grimes laughed. "Not my problem. If you want to help her, that's your business, but her hands stay tied."

WHILE GRIMES AND COMPANY had their attention on the rock bridge before them, Annja tested her bonds. Beck had tied them pretty tightly, but with a little time, she might be able to loosen them enough to do something about them.

For now, though, she was out of luck.

"I'll be right here behind you," Roux said in a whisper. "If you have trouble, I'll help."

Annja shook her head. "No, don't. I won't be able to catch myself if I slip and all I'll do is end up pulling you over with me. Someone has to keep Connolly from getting the staff."

Even as she said it, she knew Connolly wasn't her biggest concern anymore. Yes, they needed to keep the staff out of his hands, but more importantly, they needed to keep it out of Grimes's. Connolly was power-hungry, but on closer observation it seemed that the real voice behind the throne was Grimes. He was just as power-hungry as Connolly, it seemed, but when it came to ruthlessness, Grimes topped Connolly by a good half mile. The staff in Connolly's hands would be bad enough. The staff in Grimes's hands would be infinitely worse.

"Time to move," Grimes called, and the group got under way once more.

Douglas stepped out onto the footbridge. This close to the end it was several yards wide and provided a nicely stable platform to stand on. Douglas had no problem with it and waved the others out behind him as he continued across.

One by one, the others followed.

Soon everyone was on the makeshift footbridge, a

few feet apart. Annja noted that the rock underfoot had been polished smooth and care had to be taken with each step.

Before long she'd worked out an odd kind of shuffle that moved her along at a decent pace but kept her feet firmly in touch with the ground, for the most part. The group was roughly in the middle of the span when Annja heard it.

A faint, buzzing sound that seemed to be rising from below them.

She slowed, then stopped, peering over the edge into the darkness, trying to see what might be causing the sound.

"Careful…" Roux warned from a few feet back as he, too, came to a stop.

"Do you hear that?" Annja asked.

"Hear what?"

"That…noise."

Roux listened.

"What's the holdup?" Grimes called out.

Annja and Roux ignored him.

"You mean that buzzing sound?"

It was growing louder and now some of the others must have heard it, too. Several of them began looking around, trying to find the source.

Annja's thoughts whirled as she tried to remember all the plagues of Egypt, especially plague number three. She could almost hear Sister Mary Margaret's voice

droning in the back of her mind, something about...
insects?

The sound was so loud now that it was impossible
to miss.

Annja peered into the darkness, trying to see.

Something was moving down there.

A great cloud of insects erupted out of the darkness, swarming upward. They flashed passed the bewildered group on the bridge, their numbers so thick
that they blotted out the light of the headlamp Annja
wore and dimmed the powerful hand lanterns Hamilton
and Gardner carried. For a moment Annja was lost in a
sea of bugs, their humming filling her ears, the brush
of their bodies against her own like a caress, and then
they were gone. The living cloud rose swiftly into the
darkness high above.

Something crawled across her skin. She dipped her
head, trying to bring her light to bear on her own body,
and in its glow saw a few straggling gnats still making
their way across her. She shook herself, trying to knock
them loose, and mostly succeeded.

She looked for Ephraim ahead of her and then for
Roux behind. Seeing them still standing on the bridge
brought a sigh of relief. All of the others seemed to have
gotten through the experience intact, as well.

A plague of gnats.

"Keep moving!" a man called from behind her,
Grimes, if she was to guess. She started walking forward once more, following Ephraim.

They hadn't taken more than ten steps before the droning sound began again, though this time it was different—louder, deeper. It was the growl of a Harley compared to the whine of a Japanese racing bike and the sound sent a shiver through Annja's bones as she realized that whatever was coming this time was going to be worse. The gnats had been there and gone again before they could do any damage. But even something twice their size, never mind bigger, could be a real problem for them out on this little sliver of stone.

She glanced over the edge, wary of overbalancing, and saw a black mass in the darkness below.

The sound grew in volume, but now there was something familiar about it. She was certain she'd heard it before. Recognition hovered on the edge of her consciousness.

Something buzzed in front of her face, attracted no doubt to the blood still on her skin, and she shook her head, trying to make it go away.

Damned fly.

Annja froze. Flies?

She'd been in enough third-world countries to recognize the sound of a swarm of flies, but to produce a roar like that the cloud had to be enormous....

They'd never make the end of the bridge. They had seconds left, if that.

"Down!" she cried suddenly. "Everybody down! Hug the surface of the bridge and hold on tight."

Ahead of her she saw Ephraim was already in motion, lowering himself and stretching out his arms, looking for a handhold, something to lock on to to secure himself against the coming storm. A glance behind showed Roux doing the same and then Annja had no time to worry about anyone but herself.

With her hands tied behind her back and the surface of the bridge slick beneath her feet, Annja had to move slower than everyone else, for fear of overbalancing. She bent one leg, lowering herself down on her knee. Flies were starting to gather around her now.

The drone grew louder, the sound jangling her nerves, making her flinch.

With one knee down, she concentrated on lowering the other. She was suddenly thankful for all the martial-arts and sword-fighting practice she'd been getting since inheriting the sword. Her core was extremely solid and it helped her maintain control as she finally got herself onto both knees.

Now came the hard part.

Without hands to catch her, her only option was to fall on her face.

Flies were buzzing all around her now, the drone of the approaching swarm blotting out all other sounds, and Annja had only seconds left, at best. She couldn't wait any longer.

As the swarm rose up from below, Annja tipped herself down and fell forward.

38

Annja watched the rock face rush to meet her and thought, This is going to hurt.

She was right.

The stone bridge hit her square on the cheek, as she slammed against the rock with a wicked crunch. She tasted blood. And then the flies were on her with a vengeance.

She could feel them in her hair, on her face, her neck, her hands. They crawled in her ears, over her eyelids, through the blood leaking out of her nose—threatening to block her nostrils. She didn't dare open her mouth. They would have swarmed inside it in a heartbeat. They were already trying to force their way in. She could feel them pushing between her lips, their numbers grinding against her teeth. The sound around her was overwhelming, a droning hum that drove like a spike through her head, cutting off rational thought, making it impossible to think of anything at all except the cloud that swarmed around her.

Which was why it took her several seconds to realize she was moving.

At first she thought she was imagining it. With all those insects crawling over her it was no wonder she had the sensation of movement. But after another few seconds, she realized she was, indeed, moving.

Not just moving, either. Oh, no, that would be too easy. After all, she'd escaped from drowning in a vast pool of blood, narrowly missed being poisoned by the deadliest amphibians, taken captive by armed gunmen and then swarmed first by a cloud of gnats and now by flies.

She needed to have the weight of the flies sliding her toward the edge of the bridge. That was more her style, apparently.

Thank goodness Annja wasn't the type to scream, since her face was crawling with flies.

The side of her face slid over first, with Annja becoming aware of it when the hard surface of the rock was suddenly no longer pressing against her face. Flies reached the newly revealed flesh, but there was no mistaking the fact that there was no longer anything solid beneath her head.

She tried to pull back, a turtle retreating into its shell, but all that did was slide her shoulder forward and over the edge.

She shoved downward with her feet, trying to find something she could lock on to with her toes and anchor herself, to prevent her from sliding farther.

For a moment she succeeded. The toes of her right boot caught against the edge of crevasse in the stone, halting her forward momentum, but then the weight of the insects tipped the balance and Annja began sliding forward once more.

I am not going to die like this. But the truth was, she didn't see any way of stopping it. Her hands were tied too tightly to bring them around to help, her feet weren't finding purchase and her head was too full of the buzz of flies for her to think straight.

Then, out of nowhere, a hand grabbed her boot.

It was so unexpected that she did scream, the force of the air coming out of her mouth momentarily keeping her from being smothered by an influx of flies. She clamped her lips shut and fought the urge to kick back against the hand that held her.

Only her instinct for self-preservation kept her from lashing out.

Fingers had locked themselves around her calf and the pull in the opposite direction stopped her slide. She hung there, her left shoulder and the top of her head still hanging over the side of the bridge.

The person kept pulling, dragging her, until, inch by inch, the rest of her body had slid backward far enough that there was solid stone beneath her once again.

In what seemed like another miracle, the cloud of flies at last seemed to be moving on. Annja was still covered with them, but there didn't seem to be any more coming up from below and even those on her body began to take off, following their fellows into the air above like the gnats that had gone before.

Annja spat sharply several times, clearing flies from her mouth. A few violent shakes of her head removed ones that had been crawling in her hair and ears.

"You all right, Annja?"

She recognized Roux's voice and realized that it had been he who had saved her life. Somehow, even in the midst of dealing with the flies himself, he had realized that she was in trouble and had pulled himself forward on his stomach until he'd been in a position to arrest her slide.

"I'm good," she told him, then turned away and spat several more times. "Thank goodness they weren't anything bigger."

Anything bigger.

This wasn't over yet.

Her eyes snapped open even as hands grabbed her beneath her armpits and lifted her. She saw Ephraim in front of her, climbing to his feet. In front of him Douglas and Beck were already up, brushing flies off with short, sharp sweeps of their hands.

"Are you all—" Roux began, but Annja spun around, cutting him off midsentence.

"We need to get off this bridge, Roux. We need to do it now!"

"That's what we're trying to do, now let me just check—"

"We don't have time!" Even saying it aloud made her

blood turn to ice. If the pace between the first two was any indication, they had only moments.

"There were three insect plagues," she told him. "Gnats, flies and locusts!"

Locusts.

The cloud of gnats had been bad, the swarm of flies even worse. But both of those combined weren't even close to what a horde of locusts could do.

An active swarm could cover four hundred and fifty square miles and contain billions of insects. Their weight alone would be enough to carry every single one of them to their deaths.

Roux began swearing savagely in French, which let Annja know he understood, but his next words surprised Annja. "Your sword!" he cried. "Give me your sword."

For a moment she almost said no. It hadn't been that long ago that both Roux and his former apprentice, Garin Braden, had been angling to take the sword away from her and claim it as their own. Roux had been convinced the sword had the power to release him from his extended lifetime and had wanted it for the release it symbolized. Braden, on the other hand, believed something similar, but he wanted the sword to keep it safe and prevent Roux from making a rash decision they might both come to regret. The two men had done everything in their power to get Annja to relinquish the blade and, when that didn't work, had actively tried to take it from her.

That time was behind them now. They both still coveted the sword, but they had acknowledged that she was its rightful bearer and had become content to let events play out as they would.

Without even asking what he wanted it for, Annja manifested the sword, calling it to her from the otherwhere. As always it appeared fully formed in her hands. Because of her position the sword appeared standing vertically behind her back. Roux took it from her and carefully slashed through the ropes that bound her hands. Her arms ached as the blood suddenly flowed, but she knew it would pass in a moment. She glanced at the sword and sent it back before someone else saw it and she ended up with a bullet in her back.

A deep thrumming reached her ears. To Annja it sounded like a million playing cards bouncing against the spokes of a million bicycle wheels, but she knew what it really was and it was terrifying. They couldn't be caught in the open, not this time. None of them would survive.

Ephraim was staring back at them, fear on his face as the sound grew in the distance, and she gave him the best advice she could.

"Run!"

39

Not being so worried about where she put her feet allowed Annja to instinctively make the right choices and every step she made was as swift and sure as a mountain goat. Annja watched Ephraim's eyes widen as she gained on him and then he, too, turned and began rushing for the other side.

Ahead of him, Gardner and Douglas were standing like fools, staring at them charging forward. Annja had a sudden vision of them all slamming into one another at full speed and toppling over like bowling pins. To keep that from happening, she bellowed, "Run! Run!"

Just before Ephraim reached them they finally got the message, turning and taking off. Over their heads, Annja could see the end of the bridge and the entranceway to the room beyond. For all they knew that room might be another death trap, but Annja would take that possibility over certain death any day of the week.

The sound of the bugs blotted out Roux's footfalls behind her. She was tempted to look back, to make sure he was still with her. But if she slipped and fell, it was over. If she didn't topple off the bridge, she'd slow the others down and they didn't have a second to spare.

Annja caught up with Ephraim as the surface underfoot grew wider. They were almost to the end, she realized. Just a few more yards. Rather than rush past her friend, Annja swooped in behind him, linked her arm with his and used some of her momentum to help carry him the rest of the way.

Gardner and Douglas had disappeared through the entrance at the end of the bridge, and Annja and Ephraim followed suit. They found the two security team members gasping for breath inside a small antechamber. Annja left Ephraim leaning against a wall and turned back to the entrance to find Roux standing just inside, facing the way they had come. Roux was waving his hands, beckoning those still out on the bridge to hurry.

Annja peered over his shoulder and watched as first Connolly and then Grimes ran past them into the room.

That left only Hamilton and Beck.

Hamilton was taller than Beck had longer strides. He had pulled a short distance in front of the other man when disaster struck and didn't see it happen.

Annja watched as Beck's foot came down on what must have been a slippery patch of stone, saw him stumble, then fall on the bridge. For a second she thought he was going to slide right off, but he managed to stop himself from toppling over.

Annja knelt by the doors with her hands pressed tightly over her ears and still she could hear the noise, pounding at her eardrums and threatening to render her deaf.

Hamilton, unaware of his colleague's difficulty, reached the edge of the bridge and raced into the room where the others were waiting just as Beck lurched back to his feet.

Beck glanced down, blanched at whatever it was he saw and looked up again, his gaze meeting Annja's. He lurched forward on unsteady feet and for a split second she saw regret flash across his face. He opened his mouth to say something....

The locusts erupted from below, a swarm so huge, so dense, that it looked like a solid mass as it swept over him.

One minute Beck was standing there on the bridge and the next he was gone.

The locusts continued to swarm upward in what seemed like a neverending stream and Annja watched in horror from the edge of the entranceway.

If they had all been caught on that bridge...

There was no guarantee that the locusts wouldn't follow them into the room, so Connolly ordered them to continue moving. After all, there was nothing they could do for Beck. Leaving the bridge behind them, they cautiously made their way down a winding corridor until they came to another small chamber. This one seemed empty, so Grimes confirmed first with Connolly and then called a break.

Annja was just about to sit when Grimes strode across the chamber, lifted Ephraim by the lapels of his shirt and slammed him against the wall.

"What the hell is going on, Professor? I thought you said this was a fortress citadel, like Masada. A place for the royal family to use if they wanted to get away from it all. Right now all I see is one trap after another and no sign that anyone ever lived here at all. What's going on?"

Annja stepped closer, ready to kick Grimes's ass, guards or no guards, when she felt Roux stir next to her.

"I would think even an idiot like yourself could see what was happening," Roux said.

That got Grimes's attention. He dropped Ephraim and spun around, murder in his eyes.

"Excuse me?"

"I said it should be plainly obvious, even to an idiot like yourself. You're right. This isn't a citadel, it's a vault to protect the staff. And the very plagues that Aaron called down upon the land of Egypt aeons ago are guardians for what the vault is supposed to be protecting. Seems rather fitting, doesn't it?"

Grimes fumed, but didn't advance on Roux as Annja had expected. Roux might look old, but there was a presence to him and when he was angry very few men tangled with him. Grimes glanced back at Ephraim. "Plagues?"

"Yes," the professor said. "The Hebrew Scripture tells us that when the pharaoh refused to release the people of Israel from captivity in Egypt, Moses and his brother Aaron were sent to convince him otherwise. Aaron called down ten plagues with his staff to show the power of the Almighty to Pharaoh. We've already faced the first four and in their proper order—water into blood followed by plagues of frogs, gnats and flies. We've also faced one that was out of sequential order, specifically number eight, a plague of locusts."

"That leaves five more," Connolly said.

"That's correct." Ephraim counted them off on his fingers. "Number five was a disease that killed all the livestock in the land. Number six a dust-filled wind that produced boils on anyone it touched. Number seven was a massive storm full of thunder and hail. Number eight we've already encountered and number nine was a plague of darkness."

Hamilton frowned. "That's only nine. You said there were ten. What's the last one?"

"The last plague was death," Annja interjected.

Grimes was pacing back and forth. After a moment he stopped and said, "Are you telling me that we have to get through five more of these damned things before we reach the chamber where the staff is held?"

Ephraim nodded. "That's exactly what I'm telling you."

A collective groan came from the group.

"You could always turn back and forget about the

staff," Annja said. She knew Grimes and Connolly wouldn't turn back now, even if she could convince what was left of the security detail to.

Grimes spun around to face her. "Shut up! If I hear anything like that again I'll have you gagged. No one is going back now, not after what we've been through."

Turning back to Ephraim, he said, "It's your job to guide us through this, Professor. The lives of your students depend on it. So what can we expect from plague number five?"

Annja bristled at the information that the grad students who'd accompanied them on the dig had been taken hostage. She'd hoped they'd made it back to Jerusalem safely and she hadn't stopped to consider that if Ephraim had been caught they might have been, too. If they were harmed, Grimes and Connolly were going to pay.

Ephraim had been considering Grimes's question while Annja sat there fuming. "The fact that we've already faced the eighth plague, the plague of locusts, suggests that those who relocated the staff here after the fall of the Temple were more concerned with guarding the staff than they were at rolling out the plagues in order. With that in mind, I can't see we'd have to face the fifth plague at all. Unless you've got some livestock I'm not aware of?"

That earned a laugh from both Gardner and Hamilton, which, Annja realized, had probably been

Ephraim's intention. Getting some of Grimes's men on their side wasn't a bad idea.

Grimes, however, didn't find it amusing. "Oh, I'm sure I could find something to slaughter around here if necessary."

Ephraim ignored the remark. "My guess is that we're going to have to deal with either plague number six or seven next. The dust that causes boils or a storm of thunder and hail."

Lovely, Annja mused.

40

After some discussion, the decision was made to prepare themselves for the next plague on the list.

Everyone was ordered to cover any exposed skin. Pants were taped at the ankles, sleeves at the wrists. Hats and spare clothing were used to cover their heads and faces. For places that had to be exposed in order for them to keep moving, such as the skin around the eyes, large amounts of sunscreen and lip balm were applied in the hope that doing so would keep the dust away from flesh. Hands were either protected by gloves or, in Annja's and Roux's cases, generously covered in sunscreen.

No one knew how strong the wind would be when they encountered it, so Grimes ordered the group lashed together with nylon climbing rope, leaving a yard or two between them.

They took a brief rest and when they set out fifteen minutes later they were as ready as they were ever going to be.

Grimes was right; this place was never intended to

be occupied in any way, at least not the portions of it they'd seen so far. Corridors ran to dead ends. Rooms had been built one after another for no apparent reason. Staircases took them up a level only to bring them back down again five minutes later, with nothing between but empty corridors. The constant expectation that in the next corridor, in the next room, was the next trap exhausted them.

By the time they hit the Hall of Dust, as Annja later dubbed it, they had been lulled into a period of complacency, which was exactly what the designers intended.

The room was wider than the others they had passed through and at least three times as long, but that didn't immediately raise any red flags. Mal'akh hadn't really made any sense up to this point so she didn't expect it to start being logical now. It was only when she noticed a thick layer of what looked like ultrafine-grade sand beneath their feet that she became alert.

When she'd glanced about the room, it had suddenly seemed larger than before, almost twice the size. Wisps of dust were stirring and, as she watched, one of those gained more energy, becoming a small dust devil whirling above the floor. She turned and was just in time to see another one spin up and gain mass. In seconds she could see half a dozen dust devils churning, sucking dust and dirt from the floor to grow larger by the moment.

Grimes had seen it, too. "Here it comes!" he cried.

The flares were thrown to the floor to burn on their

own. Hats and makeshift scarves were pulled down or tucked in tight, sunglasses slipped on and hands shoved into pockets. Annja realized that she'd forgotten to put anything on her earlobes, but it was too late. Hopefully her hair would protect them.

No sooner had preparations been completed than a wind kicked up out of nowhere and within moments the dust on the floor was blowing like a banshee in full wail. It enveloped them while the wind screamed, but their preparations had been well thought out and they soldiered on, for the most part untouched.

In time they reached the other side of the gallery and passed through the entry into the room beyond. As Hamilton, the last in line, crossed through, the wind behind them settled as abruptly as it had begun.

They lit new flares and quickly took stock. They had survived remarkably unscathed, with only a few blisters among them where exposed skin had come in contact with the contaminant in the dust.

A few moments of rest to drink water and tend to their injuries and then they were off again, pushing deeper into the heart of the complex.

The plague of ice and hail was one of the strangest things Annja had ever encountered while underground. But the long stretch of tunnel where the darkness was absolute, where no light at all could penetrate it was perhaps more unusual underground. They came prepared to deal with what Mal'akh threw at them and each time they emerged with nothing more than a few bruises and the odd scratch or two.

It seemed they had managed to outthink those who had designed the place.

Then, almost unexpectedly, they found the room at the center of it all, the vault that held the very item they had come to find.

In the first few seconds of standing in the doorway, they didn't understand where they were. They had just come through a series of entranceways, four in all, one immediately after the other. After the final one they found themselves in a large, ornate room.

Every other room before this had been empty and it made the beauty of this one all the more stunning as a result.

The first thing they noticed were two large gold braziers on marble stands. Each held about an inch of some kind of gold liquid which, after a quick sniff, Annja recognized as lamp oil.

She had been on digs where they had found perfectly good lamp oil in tombs thousands of years old, so Annja suggested they try to light it.

Hamilton brought the burning flare close to the surface of the oil and it lit with a whoosh. The light from the brazier alone would have allowed them to see much more of the room, but the designers hadn't been content with lighting a portion of it. An interconnected series of gutters ran from that first brazier to others around the room, spreading the light in a wave to the next and the next and the next.

What the light revealed was truly magnificent.

The room was oval, with a secondary balcony running above the main floor. Columns around the periphery supported the high ceiling—six to a side, twelve in all. Between the columns stood several statues. They were of the same bearded man in flowing robes, which Annja took to be Herod. The floor was highly polished and on its surface was a complex pattern of lighter and darker stones that led across the room to where a dais stood.

On top of the dais was a wide-backed throne covered in gold and precious gems. Oddly, the throne was overshadowed by the object that rested in a waist-high glass case to its left.

The Staff of Judea.

The four-foot staff was made of polished wood and shaped like a shepherd's crook with a hook at one end. What it lacked in splendor it made up for in majesty. It threw off such an aura of power, it was hard to look away from it.

Beside her, she heard Grimes say, "I promised you we'd find it, did I not?"

"That you did, Martin," Connolly replied.

"Then it's time to claim what is yours."

The import of their conversation didn't register with Annja until Connolly pushed his way past her.

Snapped out of her daze, she snatched at Connolly's

shirt, but Grimes was suddenly there, the barrel of his pistol pushed into her back and his voice in her ear. "Uh, uh, uh. Let him go."

"But you're going to kill him," Annja hissed.

"I'm not doing anything," Grimes replied. "He's the one who forgot we still have one plague to go."

The final plague.

The death of the firstborn.

Gun in her back or not, Annja couldn't stand by and watch a man go to his death, not when she could do something about it. Grimes was looking over her shoulder, watching to see what horrible thing would happen to his employer and alleged friend.

She twisted sideways and grabbed Grimes's wrist with her left hand, pulling it forward to keep him from twisting the gun in her direction. At the same time she brought her right arm up and unleashed a savage elbow strike at Grimes's face.

She heard his nose break with a distinctive crunch.

Grimes's head snapped back with the force of the blow and he pulled the trigger instinctively. Thankfully Annja had pushed his gun arm down when she grabbed it and the shot ricocheted off the floor and spun off into the room without hurting anyone.

"Mitchell, wait!" Annja cried.

Connolly had crossed perhaps two-thirds of the distance to the dais when the shot rang out. He spun around, saw the commotion as Annja struggled against

Grimes and took a step in their direction as Annja called out a second time.

"Stay there! Don't move."

A confused look crossed his face. "What?"

"I said stay…"

It was too late.

As the sound of grinding filled the room, Annja watched Connolly look down in horror. She let her gaze follow his.

She quickly understood his fear.

41

The floor was crumbling right out from under Connolly's feet.

The section of floor he was standing on had been decorated with a mosaic of colored stones. Wide sections of darker stone bisected by interconnecting lines of lighter stone. It was like a giant tic-tac-toe board drawn on the floor. The darker sections were two, sometimes three feet wide while the lighter ones were no more than a couple of inches at most.

Now those darker sections were falling away, caving in on themselves and collapsing into the deep pit that was suddenly revealed beneath it all, leaving Connolly precariously balanced on the lattice of lighter stone.

He looked up at the rest of them gathered there in the doorway, his terror plain. His legs were shaking.

Annja held up her hands, trying to calm him down. "Don't move," she called to him. "We'll get you out of there, just don't move."

She meant it, too. It didn't matter what he had done

to them so far. If she had the means to save him, she would try. It was the right thing to do.

The fortress, however, didn't care.

The ground beneath their feet suddenly shook, throwing them all off balance.

Annja and the others braced themselves against the walls and doorway, steadying themselves until the tremor passed.

But the movement of the ground knocked Connolly's one foot off the little beam he was standing on, making him teeter over empty space for a long, terrifying moment. As he started to fall in that direction, he threw himself forward, hoping his foot would hit the next line in the lattice design and he wouldn't fall to his death.

It was a good try, too.

His foot came down squarely on the lattice line he'd been aiming for.

Then promptly skidded off the other side.

As the others looked on, Connolly flailed his arms and, screaming, fell into the hole.

For a moment all anyone could do was stare in horrified silence.

Then Connolly's voice broke the silence.

"Help!" he cried. "Help me!"

Annja didn't stop to think, she just broke into a run. She raced forward and skidded to a stop at the edge of the giant rectangle.

He wasn't hard to find. Where there had once been solid stone, now there was nothing but a giant, gaping hole in the earth over which a thin network of lattice lines was stretched. Connolly was hanging by his hands from one of those lattice lines, dangling above a sheer drop.

He wouldn't be able to hold on long.

Footsteps closed in behind Annja. She spun around and dropped into a fighting crouch, only to find Douglas skidding to a stop, his hands raised in a sign of peace.

"What can I do?" he asked.

Annja didn't hesitate. "Give me your rope," she told him as she stripped off her pack and set it on the floor next to her. When he complied, she tied one end of the rope around his waist as an anchor, tied the other end around her own and then handed him the slack.

"I'm going out after him. I'm counting on you to keep us out of the abyss if the lattice breaks beneath our combined weight."

He looked at her like she was nuts.

"I know," she told him, holding up a hand to stop whatever it was he was about to say, "but we don't have a choice. We're out of time."

As if to emphasis her point, the ground beneath their feet shook again.

Connolly's left hand slid off the thin stone he was holding on to, leaving him hanging by one arm.

"Help!" he screamed.

"Hold on!" Annja shouted back. "We're coming!"

She turned to Douglas. "Ready?"

He nodded.

Annja extended her arms out to either side and stepped out onto the lattice.

Step by step, one foot after the other, she began making her way toward Connolly.

The footing was narrow, but Annja's feet were small and she had excellent balance. As long as she kept her cool, she should be able to reach Connolly.

Provided the next quake doesn't shake us both off the edge into oblivion.

At the halfway point she paused for a second. Looking back, she saw Douglas had company; Roux, Ephraim and Hamilton had joined him. They were all armed, including Roux, which pleased Annja to no end.

Guess someone had a change of heart.

A look beyond them showed Grimes leaning against the rear wall, his head lolling to the side. He appeared to be unconscious. Apparently she'd hit him harder than she'd thought.

Or someone else followed up for me.

She carefully crossed the last ten feet separating her from Connolly. As she drew closer, she began talking to him, explaining what she was going to do.

"Mitchell, it's Annja," she said, using first names to try to keep him calm. "I've got a rope. I'm going to get as close to you as I can and tie the rope around your waist. Then I'm going to pull you up. Understand?"

Connolly didn't like the idea at all.

"No, no, no!" he cried. "Don't get any closer! The whole thing will collapse and we'll both fall!"

She hated to admit it, but he could be right. But Annja didn't see they had a choice.

She stopped a couple of feet away from Connolly at a point where a vertical lattice line crossed a horizontal one. She slowly lowered herself into a crouch, using the intersecting lines as a handhold, and stretched out across several beams.

The lattice shook for a moment, but held.

With her weight now distributed more evenly, she'd be able to bring more of the strength in her arms to bear.

Connolly's fingers were white and she could tell he didn't have much strength left.

"Hold on, Mitchell," she said. "Just another minute or so…"

Annja untied the rope from around her waist and played out some extra to work with. Holding the end of the rope in her teeth, she then slid herself forward across another gap, until she was directly above Connolly.

The beam they were both holding on to emitted a loud crack and Connolly screamed.

But it held.

"Hurry," he whispered.

Something rushed by at the edge of her vision, but she ignored it, focusing her concentration on the task before her.

With steady hands she reached out to loop the rope around Connolly's upper chest.

42

When the others rushed to save Connolly, Grimes saw his chance. He got to his feet and headed for the dais on the other side of the room, keeping to the far right edge of the room, to avoid the sort of trap Connolly had fallen.

If they'd left a firearm behind he could have ended things easily. A few quick shots to send everyone into the abyss and it would have been over. At that point all he would have had to do was retrieve the staff. Unfortunately, the chips hadn't exactly been falling in his favor lately.

Grimes had always thought of himself as the kind of man who made his own luck, however, so he supposed this was just another example of him taking the bull by the horns. If he couldn't gun them all down, he'd simply blast them with the staff. If it was a bit messier that way, so what? End result was all that mattered, right?

Right.

He drew parallel to where Douglas and the others

were acting as an anchor for their colleagues and did his best to remain hidden in the shadows of the oversize statues along the wall as he slipped past. Both Douglas and Hamilton were excellent shots. If they figured out what he was up to, he had no doubt they'd send a hail of lead in his direction.

The ground shook again, eliciting another scream from Connolly, and Grimes knew his best chance was now, while the others were occupied.

He broke into a run, charging up the outer edge of the room. With a cry of triumph, he took hold of the staff and lifted it free.

ANNJA MANAGED TO GET the rope around Connolly's upper body without much trouble and had yanked it tight just seconds before the floor went through a new set of violent contortions.

That's when Annja discovered the flaw in her plan.

She'd taken the rope from around her waist and tied it around Connolly. So when the ground started shaking again, Annja had nothing supporting her. She was forced to hang on to the lattice grimly, refusing to be knocked loose from her perch and praying that the stone didn't crumble. It was perhaps the longest thirty seconds of her life.

In front of her, Connolly finally lost his grip and dropped away from the lattice, but the men on the other end realized what had happened from the sudden yank on the rope and stopped him from falling more than a few feet.

When the ground was steady, Annja got out of the prone position she was in and climbed to her feet. Then, using the taut rope as a safety line, she nimbly made her way back to the others. Once she was clear and back on solid ground, she gave the signal for the others to pull Connolly up.

Just then, Annja was struck by a massive energy blast that picked her up and tossed her aside like a discarded piece of trash. She flew through the air and slammed into one of the statues, then crashed to the ground.

She shook her head, and when she opened her eyes, she saw Grimes on top of the dais, the Staff of Judea in one hand. Power churned the air around him—gleaming black waves of energy that matched a black light that pulsed from his eyes.

As she watched, he snarled and thrust the staff toward where the four men were fighting to haul Connolly up.

A pulse of that energy shot out of the staff, crossed the room in the blink of an eye and slammed into the group, sending Roux, Gardner, Hamilton and Ephraim spinning away and knocking Douglas flat on his back.

Without the strength of the others to support him, Connolly's weight on the other end of the rope proved too much for Douglas. He was yanked forward, the rope tightening around his waist as he was dragged inexorably toward the edge of the drop.

"Help! Help me!" he yelled.

Annja rose to her feet, intent on rushing to his aid, when another blast from the staff roared at her. She had just enough time to throw herself out of the way before the statue she'd been standing near blew into fragments.

Grimes laughed and the sound chilled her to the bone.

She glanced toward Douglas and was just in time to watch him get dragged over the edge and disappear.

Douglas's and Connolly's screams rose above Grimes's laughter.

We're in trouble.

Ephraim had been afraid of what would happen if the staff fell into the hands of a man like Grimes and now they were seeing firsthand. The black light in Grimes's eyes and the dark essence of the power he was wielding made Annja suspect that the staff was feeding off the bearer, that the dark nature of Grimes's heart was responsible for the blackness of the staff's energy. The staff was just a staff—a power source, for lack of a better term. It was the bearer who turned it into an instrument of light or one of darkness.

Grimes's soul was as black as pitch, apparently.

They had to get that staff away from him.

The only way to do that was to get close enough to take it away.

The chatter of a semiautomatic rifle filled the room. Roux was in a crouch, the gun he'd snatched from the floor in hand, sending a blistering wave of fire directly at Grimes.

To keep from being gunned down, Grimes ducked behind the throne for cover.

"Now, Annja!" Roux roared over the din, having apparently come to the same conclusion Annja had.

Annja knew instinctively that they were only going to get one chance at this and so she didn't hesitate. She called her sword and ran for the dais.

A second gun added its chatter to Roux's. From its short, controlled bursts, Annja assumed it was Hamilton. She didn't think Ephraim had that kind of discipline with a gun.

The gunfire was forcing Grimes to keep his head down, so Annja managed to get most of the way to the dais before instinct told her it was time to get under cover.

She dove behind the nearest statue just as Grimes decided to fight back.

He came out from behind the throne with the staff already extended. The amount of time a person possessed the staff must be a factor in its use—he already seemed to be able to use it more evenly. This time Grimes sent multiple bursts of black fire across the floor at Roux and Hamilton simultaneously. Annja heard one of them scream.

She rushed along the narrow space between the columns and the wall until she was parallel with the dais. A quick glance around the statue she was huddled behind showed her that Grimes was standing on the top step of the dais, staff in hand, flinging more energy blasts at Annja's companions as he laughed at their attempts to strike him.

Annja gauged the distance in her head and figured she had to cross fifteen feet to reach Grimes. All without getting blasted to pieces.

Roux and Hamilton weren't going to be able to hold out much longer with such limited cover. Eventually Grimes was going to hit them dead-on.

Taking a deep breath, Annja spun out from behind the statue and charged straight at Grimes.

She knew she was in trouble right away. Grimes turned toward her, smiling, and she realized that he'd known where she was—had waited her out until she was so close he couldn't miss.

Annja's feet pounded the floor as she raced for the dais.

Grimes brought the staff up and pointed it at her head. It pulsed with energy.

A wave of energy burst from the tip and rushed toward her, moving so quickly that all she had time to do was thrust out her sword.

To both their astonishments, the energy blast hit the sword and peeled apart like a balloon suddenly popped.

A gunshot rang out and Grimes jerked as the bullet passed though the fleshy part of his shoulder. As Annja drew closer he changed his grip on the staff and swung at her head.

As the staff came whistling toward her, she stepped up and blocked it with the blade of her sword. For a second, the two weapons were locked together and Annja seized the moment. She snatched the knife from her belt with her free hand and slashed at Grimes's exposed arm.

The blade barely made a scratch.

But in this case, a scratch was more than enough. She hadn't had time to clean the blade after her encounter with the frogs back in the second-plague room and it was still coated with the toxins from their flesh and blood. All it took to transfer those toxins to the bloodstream was the smallest scratch.

Like the one she'd just given Grimes.

This close, Annja saw Grimes's eyes widen as he felt the poison enter his bloodstream. His face broke out in a sweat and a moment later his body jerked as the neurotoxins went to work on the nerve junctures within his system.

Grimes's hands spasmed with surprising force and the staff fell to the floor of the dais.

His body was no longer acting under his control, it seemed. Neurons were firing everywhere, sending him into a series of fits and starts that would have made a medieval torturer proud. He jerked and twisted and convulsed, until finally he collapsed into unconsciousness.

Annja prodded him with her sword, but he didn't react. His breathing was very shallow and she didn't think he'd live out the hour.

The others were suddenly there with her on the dais,

telling her that she'd not only stopped Grimes but found the Staff of Judea, too.

The staff.

She turned and walked over to it.

This close, Annja could feel the power coming off it. The air around it seemed to react, as well; there was a slight shimmer around the entire length of the staff, making it difficult to see clearly, reminding her of the visual distortion on a hot day in the desert.

She bent and reached out for it, when a voice rang out from the balcony above.

"Stop!"

43

They all—herself, Roux, Ephraim, even Hamilton—
spun to face the direction the voice was coming from.

Men, dressed in the black desert robes Annja had
last seen on the horsemen who had rescued her from
Grimes, lined the balcony. Annja quickly counted at
least twenty-five of them and she had no doubt there
were more on the balcony directly above her. Several
carried curved blades similar to those Roux had given
to his hired hands, but Annja's trained eye picked out
subtle differences between the two sets of blades almost
immediately. Annja had no doubt that the swords she
was looking at were the originals the others had been
modeled after. In addition to the blades, a few also carried modern firearms. She recognized what looked to
be a Soviet-issue AK-47, an Israeli Uzi, even an American M4 carbine remarkably similar to the one in Hamilton's hands.

The muzzles of the guns were pointed at her party.
Annja glanced at Roux. Were the newcomers what

was left of the mercenaries he had hired? He shook his head ever so slightly, indicating that was not the case.

Annja opened her arms, holding them out at the sides of her body to show she wasn't a threat in any way. "My name is Annja Creed. Who are you and what do you want with us?"

He said something in return.

Annja stared up at the speaker. She didn't recognize the language he was speaking, never mind understand what he was saying. She frowned; it sounded like Hebrew, but the accents and emphasis seemed to be in the wrong places.

Ephraim, however, practically began jumping up and down the moment he heard it. He grabbed Annja's sleeve and, pulling her close, whispered, "If I'm right that's a local dialect that hasn't been spoken commonly since the fall of the temple. Let me try to talk to him, see if we can find a way to understand each other."

Annja nodded. It wasn't as if she had a better idea.

Ephraim cleared his throat and then said something in a language that sounded close to the one the other man had used.

Close but not quite.

The visitor said something sharp in reply, then repeated it, as if teaching Ephraim the proper way to say it.

Ephraim smiled sheepishly, nodded and then tried again. The two men traded several remarks back and forth, with Ephraim growing more and more excited.

At last he turned to Annja and said, "I was right. It is a dialect not used very often, so it took me a little while to work it out."

"So you think the two of you can communicate now?"

Ephraim nodded. "Oh, yes. I might get an occasional word wrong but that shouldn't be too much of a problem."

Unless that one word completely changes the nature of the statement. There's a world of difference between "I love you" and "I hate you," that was for sure.

She glanced at the armed men on the balcony. "All right," she told Ephraim. "Give it a go."

Eagerly Ephraim spoke, pointing to himself in the process. Annja heard him say his name a couple of times, and then he was clearly introducing all of them.

When the newcomer replied, Ephraim's eyes grew wide and he translated what he was hearing.

"He says his name is Jephthah, leader of the Giborrim, the men of valor whom the Lord entrusted to guard the instrument of His righteousness. This is amazing, Annja!"

It didn't take an archaeologist to understand that when Jephthah mentioned the "instrument of righteousness" he was referring to the staff. Unlike Ephraim, Annja wasn't thrilled with this latest development. She hadn't missed that none of the Giborrim, if that was indeed who they really were, had lowered their weapons.

Jephthah waited until Ephraim had finished translating before he continued. This time when he spoke, he went on longer. Whatever he was saying must not have been very good, for Ephraim's excitement had abated by the time Jephthah was finished.

Ephraim turned to her and the others and said, "Because we are outside the faith, the Giborrim believe we have spoiled this holy sanctuary by our presence here. That each and every breath we take here further contaminates it, like meat left to rot in the summer sun."

It was hard to see the Giborrim leader's expression from this distance, but the crossed arms and hard stance told her that he wasn't the type who was interested in forgiveness.

"Tell him—"

Ephraim cut her off. "He went on to say that because we have violated the holy space, our lives would be forfeit—"

"Forfeit my ass," Hamilton said, surging to his feet.

This, in turn, caused Jephthah's men to surge forward. Those with projectile weapons, traditional or modern, aimed them at the former Marine.

"Wait, wait!" Ephraim yelled, holding up his hands and putting himself in front of Hamilton, trying to shield the larger man. He shouted something presumably in ancient Hebrew to the men on the balcony.

At a gesture from their leader, the Giborrim backed down.

Hamilton did the same.

Ephraim wiped at the sweat on his forehead. "But

he, Jephthah," he told his companions in English, "is willing to let us live, provided we turn something over to him."

"What do we have that he wants?" Hamilton asked.

The sinking feeling in Annja's gut told her she already knew the answer.

"He wants Annja's sword."

44

Her sword.

Annja stared at Ephraim, so shocked by Jephthah's demand that for a moment she couldn't find her voice.

Everyone in the room had seen her pull that sword out of midair and use it to defend herself against Grimes. The Giborrim must have been watching, as well. If she hadn't called her sword, she and everyone else in the room with the exception of Grimes would have died.

She had been wondering what she was going to do about Hamilton, Gardner and Ephraim knowing her secret when she got out of here, but now it seemed that problem was going to take a backseat.

If she gave away the sword, would it still be hers?

She didn't know. She had tried to give it away previously. But the thing hadn't exactly come with an instruction manual. The sword had pretty much claimed her the night it had been reassembled and she'd felt, well, bonded to it ever since.

She'd always felt that it was more than just inanimate

worked steel, but just how *much* more, she didn't know. Certainly there'd been times while wielding it that she'd felt its presence in the back of her mind, urging her on, lifting her to newer and better heights.

Thinking quickly she said to Ephraim, "Ask him to come down to speak with me."

Annja watched with bated breath as Jephthah thought it over for a moment before nodding and issuing instructions to the men around him. They drew back away from the edge of the balcony, out of sight. No doubt on their way down to where Annja and the others waited.

Think quickly!

"Annja, you can't seriously be—"

She held up a hand, palm out, shushing Roux. She needed to concentrate.

She knew from experience that she could hand over the sword and not have it immediately disappear, provided she was still in the same room. That complicated any move to try to trick the Giborrim leader. The minute she and the others left the room, the sword would vanish back into the otherwhere. With the Giborrim far more knowledgeable about the fortress's layout, they'd be able to run them to ground.

They wouldn't get another chance if that happened.

Better make it good, then.

The Giborrim entered the room through two hidden doorways on either side of the room. Annja hadn't even known they were there. The group flowed together to form a cordon around their leader and came forward as a unit. When they were about ten feet from the foot of the dais, the group stopped, the cordon splitting open to allow the leader to go on alone.

He met Annja near the base of the dais.

"Hello, Jephthah," she said in English.

"It is a pleasure to meet you, Annja Creed."

He lagged a little on the pronunciation of Annja, carrying the *n*'s too long, but his English was quite good all the same.

Annja had suspected as much. Jephthah seemed like a capable leader and what leader worth their salt doesn't take the time to study and know their enemies?

"We would like to resolve this peacefully," she said.

He nodded. "I, too, would like that, Annja Creed. However, you and our companions have broken our sacred law and righteousness must be satisfied. Were we to let you go, we would have no way of assuring ourselves that you would not return, perhaps with greater numbers or more force, to take that which is not yours."

The Staff.

He watched her for a moment, then said, "Your sword. It is a holy weapon, yes?"

Annja answered without thinking. "Yes."

Almost immediately she questioned her answer. Joan of Arc had believed herself to be called by God. And the sword prompted Annja to act as a force of good, protecting the defenseless and the innocent.

But something could be good without being holy, couldn't it?

So was the sword a holy artifact?

She didn't know.

And upon reflection, she decided she was perfectly okay with that.

Jephthah nodded and asked, "May I see it, please?"

Annja called the sword.

It sprang into her hands, the blade upright between her and Jephthah. With just a flick of her wrist, his life would be forfeit.

From the mischievous look in his eyes, he recognized it, as well. It was a test.

Okay, I can play that game, too.

She reversed the blade, then extended the hilt toward the Giborrim leader.

"Please," she said. "Take it. Decide for yourself if it's holy or not.

He reached out and took the sword from her.

FROM WHERE HE LAY on the floor near the dais, Grimes watched Annja hand that sword of hers to the Israeli standing in front of her. His hatred for her filled his heart.

She had bested him, not once, not twice, but three times now. She had escaped from him in the desert, had derailed his original attempt to kill that idiot Connolly and had then poisoned him when he'd tried to claim the staff for his own. He let his hatred pour fire into his blood, let it provide the strength he needed to do what had to be done.

Annja Creed must die.

He was surprised he was still alive. He'd recognized the toxin from the way his body had reacted to it and he knew very few people survived dart frog poison. Perhaps the staff had protected him from its worst effects.

Everyone's attention was on Annja, and Grimes made use of the opportunity afforded him, turning his head slightly to take in the positions of those around him. He could see that traitor, Hamilton, Gardner and the old fool, Roux, standing next to each other off to the side. The professor was closer, near where the staff had fallen when Annja had struck him down, but Grimes didn't care. He would deal with the professor after he killed the others. Then he would take up the staff.

But first, he was going to kill Annja Creed.

He turned his head a little more and saw the instrument of his salvation.

ANNJA SAW JEPHTHAH'S eyes light up as he took the sword and she wondered what it was he was seeing as he accepted it from her hand.

That's when the first shot rang out.

Annja spun around.

Grimes was sitting up on the dais, the pistol he'd dropped earlier back in his hand and pointing to where Roux had been standing next to Hamilton. Even as Annja registered the sight of Hamilton's body being thrown back against the wall from the impact of the first shot's bullet, Grimes pulled the trigger a second time and red blossomed across Roux's shirt before he, too, was thrown backward.

"No!" Annja cried, and tried to call her sword back to her.

Grimes spun around, leveling the gun at Annja even as she began to wonder if the sword had chosen a new bearer.

The solid hilt slapped into her hand. For now, at least, she was the only bearer the sword would have. But if she didn't live through the next few seconds it wouldn't matter one way or the other.

Peripherally she could see, and feel, the Giborrim warriors swinging up their weapons, ready to take on this new threat. Annja knew, with the surety of those who have embraced their own death, the warriors would never get a shot off in time.

As Grimes's finger began to tighten on the trigger, Annja brought her sword arm back over her head, her muscles tensing for the throw. It was going to have to be very, very good....

She never got the chance to find out.

Over Grimes's shoulder she watched Ephraim rear up, the Staff of Judea in his hand. His eyes blazed with silver fire, his hands shone with holy light, and for just an instant he wasn't holding a staff of wood but one made of light.

He swung the staff like a major league baseball player and connected with Grimes's skull.

There was a sharp knock, like the sound you get

when a player has hit the ball squarely on target. Grimes dropped like a stone, never having had the chance to pull the trigger.

45

For a moment Ephraim stood there, staring at them all, and then he collapsed facedown on the dais.

"Ephraim!" Annja cried, turning to rush to his side, only to be stopped as Jephthah grabbed her arm in a viselike grip.

"Wait!" he said. "It is not safe. Your friend has seen the face of the Almighty. He will not recognize you. Let my people handle it."

Without waiting for an answer Jephthah shouted instructions in his mother tongue, and a dozen or so of his warriors ran across the room and up onto the dais. Rather than work on Ephraim where he lay, they lifted him over their heads and raced back down the steps to disappear through the doors they'd entered.

"Hey, wait!" she shouted, but Jephthah stopped her again. This time with only his voice.

"Your other friends need you more, I think." He nodded to where Roux, Gardner and Hamilton lay bleeding on the polished stone.

Annja snarled at him and then ran to help.

When she looked up ten minutes later, Jephthah was gone.

THANKFULLY NEITHER ROUX nor Hamilton were seriously injured. The bullet that had hit Roux glanced off the side of his hard head, knocking him unconscious and leaving a shallow furrow along the side of the head that would leave a scar. Hamilton, on the other hand, had taken a shot to his shoulder, but the bullet had passed through without breaking up and once Annja stopped the bleeding his biggest concern was keeping it clean from infection.

Annja wouldn't leave Ephraim behind and so the group remained where they were, dozing more or less fitfully. Annja was startled from sleep when she heard her name being called.

Ephraim stood halfway across the room, dressed in the robes of the Giborrim, beckoning to her.

Even from here, she could see the strange gleam still in his eyes.

She got up and went to meet him.

"How are you?" he asked, once they were standing opposite each other and out of earshot of the others.

She stared into those silvery eyes for only a moment and then had to look away. She hadn't seen anything of her friend in those eyes.

"I'm fine," she said. "Hamilton needs a hospital, though."

And so, apparently, do you, she thought, but didn't say it.

Ephraim heard her just the same.

"I don't need a hospital," he told her. He was quiet a moment, then added, "I'm no longer the Ephraim you knew, Annja. At least, not just the Ephraim you knew. I am more than that now. I've changed."

You can say that again.

"I've changed," he said, and this time he smiled.

It was creepy as hell, but somehow that smile reassured her. It had been Ephraim's smile and that told her they weren't in any danger from this man.

"I've spoken to Jephthah. He's agreed to let you go. Says it is unjust to hold those who were instrumental in saving his life, and I agree with him."

"That's great, Ephraim! Let's get our stuff and get out of here."

Ephraim studied her, his head cocked to one side. "I'm not going home with you, Annja."

For a long while neither of them said anything.

Then Annja said, "Yeah, okay. I understand."

And oddly, the truth was she did. Ephraim had been touched by something and would never be the same. She knew what that was like, and she couldn't imagine him returning to the life he had known.

She certainly hadn't, not really.

"You'll be okay?"

He nodded. "Better than I've ever been, Annja. I wish I could tell you what it's like, but I don't have the words. Maybe someday I'll find you and tell you what I can. And perhaps you can share the story of your sword with me in turn."

Annja smiled, but she felt sad, lonely. "I'd like that."

After that, there wasn't much else to say. At Ephraim's summons Jephthah's men returned, helped them gather their gear and then led them all back to the surface.

Henshaw was waiting for them beside the helicopter. He told Annja how he'd been attacked from behind just after landing, had spent the day in captivity without ever seeing his captors and had been released just moments before she and the others had showed up. He obviously noticed Ephraim's silvery eyes, did a double take, but didn't say anything.

Annja gave a point to whoever had conducted Henshaw's British butler training. Ignoring eyes that glow with inner fire? That was impressive.

They loaded everyone aboard the chopper, including Daniels and Johnson who'd been guarding the entrance, then gave Ephraim and his Giborrim comrades time to get clear of the rotors before Henshaw fired it up. When he'd come to a few hours before, Hamilton had told Annja where Ephraim's graduate students were being held captive and she intended to stop on the way home to make sure of their safety. After that, it would be a night in Jerusalem to get some much-needed rest and then a flight back to New York and a return to her job as cohost of *Chasing History's Monsters*.

It was funny, but she was looking forward to whatever assignment her producer Doug Morrell sent her on next. Right about now hunting the rabid dog men of upper Botswana sounded just fine. She'd had enough of long-lost treasures for the time being.

Later that night, she would find the copy of the scroll translations Ephraim had slipped into her backpack and would take the time to reconsider. But for now, she was content to just sit back and enjoy the ride.

* * * * *

The Executioner®
Don Pendleton's

DOUBLE CROSS

A Haitian gang turns the streets of Miami into a death zone.

Dozens are killed in a bloody attack outside a West Palm Beach courthouse when two Haitian gang leaders break out their brethren as a show of power over the city. Mack Bolan is sent in to neutralize the situation, but finds that things have escalated. While the police department and local residents are too frightened to fight back, Bolan is not—especially after finding the battered remains of the gang's innocent victims. The leaders of this crime ring may have risen from the streets, but the Executioner is prepared to send them to the depths of hell.

GOLD EAGLE®

Available April wherever books are sold.

JAMES AXLER

DEATH LANDS®

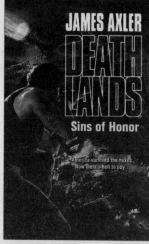

Sins of Honor

America survived the nukes. Now there's hell to pay....

New Hampshire is rich with big game, more than enough to feed Ryan and the other hungry survivors. But claims to a fallen elk get ugly and Ryan is forced to chill another hunter, the self-proclaimed king of the Granite Highlands, over the meat. Soon the hunters become the hunted as the dead man's widow gives chase, armed with predark tanks and heavy artillery. As the kill zone widens across cannibal-ridden lava fields, Ryan and his group search for leverage in the merciless landscape.

Available May wherever books are sold.